By the Grace of the Gods

Roy
Illustrations by Ririnra

BY THE GRACE OF THE GODS VOLUME 2
by Roy

Translated by Mana Z.
Edited by Nathan Redmond
Layout by Leah Waig
English Cover & Lettering by Jordan Voon

Copyright © 2017 Roy
Illustrations by Ririnra

First published in Japan in 2017
Publication rights for this English edition arranged through Hobby Japan, Tokyo.

Find more books like this one at www.j-novel.club!

President and Publisher: Samuel Pinansky
Managing Editor (Novels): Aimee Zink
QA Manager: Hannah N. Carter
Marketing Manager: Stephanie Hii

ISBN: 978-1-7183-5381-7
Printed in Korea
First Printing: February 2021
10 9 8 7 6 5 4 3 2 1

Contents

Chapter 2 Episode 1
An Afternoon Off 11

Chapter 2 Episode 2
Magic Practice 23

Chapter 2 Episode 3
Invitation Received 33

Chapter 2 Episode 4
Abandoned Mine Investigation 41

Chapter 2 Episode 5
True Alchemy 50

Chapter 2 Episode 6
Afternoon Expedition and a Gift 60

Chapter 2 Episode 7
Morgan Trading Company 70

Chapter 2 Episode 8
Large-Scale Subjugation Request 81

Chapter 2 Episode 9
An Average Adventurer 89

Chapter 2 Episode 10
Monster Subjugation Break Time 101

Contents

Chapter 2 Episode 11
Unruly Adventurers 114

Chapter 2 Episode 12
Monster Subjugation at the Mines, End of Day 1 122

Chapter 2 Episode 13
Report 128

Chapter 2 Episode 14
Monster Subjugation at the Mines, Day 2 136

Chapter 2 Episode 15
Inquiry 144

Chapter 2 Episode 16
Group Battle 151

Chapter 2 Episode 17
Fight Over, Fight Ongoing 158

Chapter 2 Episode 18
Return Home 167

Chapter 2 Episode 19
Business Discussions (Part 1) 179

Chapter 2 Episode 20
Business Discussions (Part 2) 188

Contents

Chapter 2 Episode 21
Instant Decision   197

Chapter 2 Episode 22
Store Setup 1   208

Chapter 2 Episode 23
Store Setup 2   216

Chapter 2 Episode 24
Store Setup 3   225

Chapter 2 Episode 25
Store Setup 4   236

Extra Story
The Ones Left Behind and the Signs of Change   245

∾ Chapter 2 Episode 1 ∾
An Afternoon Off

The next day.

I opened my eyes to see the sun's rays shining into the room.

Ahh, what a good night's sleep... It's been a while since I pulled an all-nighter... The sun seems to be fairly high in the sky, too... Wait, the sun's high in the sky? ...Oh no!

"Good morning, Master Ryoma."

"Sebas, what time is it?"

"Just before noon. You must have been exhausted, since you rested for quite a long time. Would you like to eat?"

"I appreciate the offer, but I have to go to the guild. I'll eat once I'm back."

"As you wish, then."

I got myself ready quickly and headed for the guild. There was no time left... I guess I had only one option here.

"Enshroud my body and divert attention — Conceal."

I set up a concealment barrier around my body to hide myself, then activated the neutral magic Physical Enhancement. Magic energy wrapped around my body, allowing me to leap up to the roof of a nearby building with my enhanced physical ability. Then I ran along the rooftops as a shortcut. I would use the space magic Teleport whenever I ran out of places to step, allowing me to run towards the guild in pretty much a straight line.

"Excuse me."

I burst into the guild in a fluster, and was led to a room where everyone else was already gathered.

"You're finally here, Ryoma. That makes everyone."

"Sorry for the wait."

"You're just in time. Don't worry about it. Now, it's time to talk rewards!"

The allocation of rewards was conducted, and I received the original reward for the cleaning job of 3 medium silver coins as well as 30 small gold coins. Everyone else each received 10 small gold coins.

"Hey, hold on, this is rather generous."

"Ain't it, though? We'll take what we're given, but you do know we were just on lookout duty, right?"

"Isn't the reward a little too high? I understand there was a risk of contracting the epidemic, but seeing as we didn't do anything directly with it, just half of this should be appropriate."

"Nope, that amount is correct. And the reason for that is… Ryoma."

"Yes?"

"According to you, the epidemic in that pit toilet was the Idake virus, right?"

"Yes. I verified it with Appraisal, so there's no mistaking it."

"In which case, I've received information that it was a fairly severe situation. I know an old lady who's familiar with this stuff… She said its mortality rate was relatively low for an epidemic, but it spreads easily and has awful aftereffects that leave survivors without mobility, rendering them as good as dead. That's why the reward is this high. Even if the mortality rate is low, the elderly and children would be still susceptible to death, and those who survive wouldn't be able to work anymore."

Everyone broke out into a cold sweat at those words. It really was awful... Depending on the severity of the aftereffects, being unable to work meant being unable to make a living. That would have been fatal in this world, where insurance and government protection didn't exist. In the end, people would die of starvation.

"Thank goodness it was stopped early, nya..."

"In a way, it's more terrifying than an epidemic with a high mortality rate..."

"At least if you died, that would be the end of it. But if surviving meant living in hell, then..."

"The public office has received a good scolding over this incident, and several people, including the head, have been arrested. Those that remained were making a clamor about how to go about cleaning the communal toilet pits in the future."

"You can't leave them to the guys from the slums?"

"Unfortunately not. The head of the public office was fired for withholding pay over this incident, but they no longer trust that they'll be paid the correct amount. And most of the guys from the slums have found new work already. Unlike other towns, we're close to the mines so there's no lack of employment if you're willing to get your hands dirty doing labor. If they can get money elsewhere, they're not going to bother with the work cleaning the toilet pits. The fault was with the public office this time, so it's not like they're in a position to make demands about quitting working for them. They've basically given up on hiring from the slums."

"So what will you do? It was lucky that Ryoma noticed it this time, but we can't go through this every time."

"That's true... Actually, it was forced upon the guild yesterday — they said they'd pay us to deal with it. I guess I have no choice but to make those who regularly fail at jobs or break contracts to do so as a penalty..."

"We'll entrust that to you. I'm sure you'll come up with a solution."

"Easy for you to say…"

"It's okay, I'll keep accepting the requests while I'm in town, so please use that time to think of a plan."

"That would be great."

"Nya? Did you come from another town, Ryoma?"

Come to think of it, I hadn't had the chance to tell everyone yet since I was immediately on the job. I explained the series of events that led me to Gimul Town.

"Living alone in the forest at eight years old? How reckless…"

"Will you return to the Forest of Gana?"

"I'm not sure… I'm very fond of the house in the forest I inhabited for three years… But I may end up living in the forest around here instead."

"No, if you want to live nearby you should stay in town. Why would you go out of your way to live in the forest?"

"I can make a house from magic and hunt for food. It actually makes for a pretty comfortable life, you know? I don't need any money either."

"Ryoma, I believe thou may still be too young to discard the world like that."

"That's true… I did realize that too, faintly."

"Well, think carefully about it so you don't end up having regrets. We'll be grateful to have you around, but there's no need to stay in this town longer than you're comfortable with. You should live freely, the way you want to. At any rate, the guys involved in the embezzlement this time had their assets seized on top of being fired, and those subordinates who didn't speak up had their pay deducted. That leaves more money to put into the town's maintenance fees. In the worst case, we can use the money to hire help as needed. Now, I've handed you your rewards and said my piece. There's one last message I have to pass on. The day after tomorrow, a large request will be coming in. There's a mine that's closing this year, but it's pretty much been abandoned since last year. Many monsters have nested inside the mine. They're all small fry, but the area is large so we're recruiting a number of adventurers. I hope you'll all participate with enthusiasm. That's all, dismissed!"

With the meeting over, everyone went their own ways, and I returned to the inn.

The young miss and her family were waiting for me at the inn. Apparently they were waiting so we could all have lunch together. I thanked them and took my seat, when the young miss started talking to me.

"Ryoma, would you like to train together?"

"Why so suddenly?"

"I'm going to start practicing magic from today. That's why I thought it would be nice for you to join, too."

"Actually, the trip we're on right now is also meant to be practical experience for Elia."

According to them, the Jamil ducal family had a custom of sending their children on a journey once they reached a certain age, sometimes letting them become an adventurer if they so wished.

"Going on a journey to widen your views and knowledge is a good thing. However, there are many things required to do that, like having the strength to protect oneself. We could have just sent escorts with her, but that would have been restrictive. With no hard work put into it, there would only be half as much to gain. That is why our goal is to give Elia the strength to protect herself."

15

"Even if she didn't go on that journey, there would still be times where she may need to participate in exterminations of monsters and bandits in our domain."

Reinbach and Reinhart explained, surprising me a little.

"Even the young miss?"

"The participation of a noble in an extermination increases the scale, you know? And it isn't limited to Elia. We have to show the public that we're protecting our domain, and we also raise morale this way. That's why she needs strength to an extent."

I see. And gender differences didn't matter when it came to magic, either.

"That's why I'll be attending school in the capital beginning this year, studying and learning magic. Which is why I wanted to gain some experience before that."

"I see, so that's why you came here."

"That's right. I was training from morning until just earlier, and I'll be continuing in the afternoon. Would you like to participate in that training too, Ryoma?"

…Yeah, it sounded like a good opportunity. I had promised to teach her how to play with magic before, and I would love to learn things myself if it wasn't a bother.

When I said that, they readily agreed to me joining the afternoon training session. With the training being for magic, they were apparently holding it in a rocky area roughly 20 minutes out of town by horse carriage.

■ ■ ■

After lunch.

The carriage arrived at the rocky area, where Jill was waiting for us.

"We've been waiting for you, young miss. You too, Ryoma. It must have been a tiring three days."

"Thank you too, Jill. I heard you've been busy yourself."

"Fairly so."

"Come on, let's begin already!"

The young miss said with giddy impatience. She seemed to be really looking forward to playing with magic.

"By the way, which elements can you use? I'll need to know so that I can teach you how to play as well."

"I specialize in fire and ice magic. I have lots of magic energy, so if I train more I'll be able to fire lots of powerful magic."

The way she said "lots of powerful magic" made it sound like her strength was in firepower. And in fire and ice magic, of all things…

"Is there a problem?"

"Water and earth magic are safer than fire and ice, so there won't be as much that you can play with."

"You certainly wouldn't want to play with fire in a forest."

"Forest fires are no joke."

Hughes and Jill muttered from where they were standing at a distance. They were exactly right. Though the least favorable element to play with was actually poison, in my opinion.

"For fire magic, I can only teach you this. *Darkness. Little Fire Flower.*"

After I used the dark elemental magic Darkness to darken the space above my hand, I pointed using my index finger and illuminated the darkness with little sparks of fire for several seconds. It was a magic based on sparklers.

"It's beautiful."

"That's right."

"Oh, it's gone."

"It feels a little sad to see it end."

Well, sparklers had that effect too. There was no point to this magic other than being pretty to look at. I wanted to recreate large fireworks too, but my magic wasn't quite good enough for that yet.

As for ice elemental magic, there was ice skating and ice sculptures to play with. After making the first piece of ice, magic was only used to keep it cold, but the scale was rather large. And while I could make ice sculptures with my experience as a part-time sculpting assistant in my past life, it took time to learn and do well. Depending on what was being sculpted, stamina would be required to stack the blocks of ice, and there was a risk in getting hurt if the stack collapsed. Although that was what made the pay good... And it also kept the cave cool when I left it in the corner on a hot day.

Something smaller-scaled would have been making a lens from ice and using it to gather light and spark a fire, but that honestly wasn't something that could be enjoyed for very long... If you wanted a spark, it would be a hundred times faster to just use fire magic anyway... Hmm...

"How about water, then? I'm not good at it, but I can use water magic too."

"In that case, there's something. For example... *Bubbly Water.*"

I joined the fingertips of both hands and created water inside the circle. But that water was more viscous than normal water, creating a membrane across my hand. I blew gently at it to create a bubble the size of a head and released it into the air.

19

If I used the wind magic *Breeze* to blow a stronger wind at the remaining membrane, countless smaller bubbles would float upwards.

The clear blue sky could be seen in the background. Nothing obstructed the sunlight shining on the bubbles drifting softly through the windless air. The light reflecting off the surface sparkled like iridescent starlight. Eventually, they popped and disappeared.

"Oh my, that was interesting. They looked like soap bubbles."

"It's beautiful."

The water that could create bubbles seemed to be a hit with the women. Soap was used by the general population, but it was expensive so they wouldn't use it on this. The men looked like they enjoyed it as well.

"This is a water magic that gives the water viscosity. For example… *Water. Wave.*"

I used my hand as a cup to pour water in, then moved it with a different magic.

"*Wave* is a basic magic that creates ripples on the water surface, but this is done by using water magic on water magic to make movement. That's why when you practice it… here!"

With a shout, I launched the water in my hand up high. Normally, gravity would bring the water back down, but it didn't fall at all. Everyone around me looked up to see the sphere of water floating above my head. Of course, I was using the magic that moved water to keep it there.

Since there was a water magic called Waterball that launched a sphere of water as an attack, the reactions around me were still lukewarm. That's why this was only the start.

"Ooh!"

I moved the water until the shape changed into that of a goldfish, causing light voices of surprise around me. After three years of boredom, my water goldfish was accurate down to the last scale. When I moved it through the air while bending it periodically...

"It looks like it's swimming through the air!"

"How clever."

Everyone applauded me, but that just made me feel shy.

"Well, this is just one way of using water. When I was thinking of a way to put magic into the water for viscosity, I made the Bubbly Water earlier. I imagined connecting the individual droplets of water together."

"Like this? *Bubbly Water.*"

The young miss was able to make a water viscous enough to create a membrane between her hands. But it would break as soon as she blew lightly at it.

"Use a little more water elemental magic and imagine the water being like a sticky slime's sticky solution."

She was already halfway there, so I tried giving a more concrete example.

Then, the young miss eagerly released her magic energy as she chanted the spell.

"*Bubbly Water.*"

This time, the water that was created was clearly more viscous. She blew into the ring she made with her fingers and a new bubble danced into the sky.

"I did it!"

"The size will vary greatly depending on how hard you blow, and with a little more practice and magic control you can even do this."

Once again, I made another bubble — this time with more magical energy. I stopped it at the size of a basketball and made it float before me... then lightly smacked it.

"Here!"

"Huh?!"

The bubble distorted heavily, but didn't pop as it floated over to the young miss. The young miss, who had been watching with interest nearby, caught the bubble and juggled it from hand to hand.

"This one... didn't disappear like the others."

"If you use more magic energy, the bubble becomes strong enough to stay intact even if you touch it. It will pop under a large enough force and disappear eventually, though."

For the record, this bubble was purely made from water, so it was safe for both humans and the environment. Even if a young child ate one, it wouldn't hurt them at all.

"For some reason, it's starting to look like a slime to me."

The young miss poked the bubble and gleefully watched it wobble.

Seeing her enjoy herself made teaching her worthwhile. If I had a chance in the future, I'd teach her some other elemental magic tricks too.

⇜ Chapter 2 Episode 2 ⇝
Magic Practice

"Now, shall we begin?"

After playing with the bubbles for a while, it was time to start today's training.

"Young miss, you'll be continuing with your magic control lesson from this morning. Master Ryoma, do you have any requests?"

"I'd like to learn attack magic for each of the elements. Like I mentioned previously at the church, I've barely used any attack magic."

"That was right. In that case, the best person would be…"

"Me, right?"

Sebas' gaze landed on Camil. It seemed like he would be in charge of teaching me.

"Ryoma can use all elements, is that correct? I can use all the lower elemental magics, as well as lightning and ice magic. I can't teach higher elemental magics like poison and wood, but I know the basics of everything else."

"Is that so? Then I will be in your care, Camil."

"Same here."

"Then, Ryoma. We will see you later."

The young miss would be training elsewhere, which the wife informed me of before they left.

I saw them off in confusion — weren't we going to train in the same place?

When I asked Camil, he answered, "It's for safety, I guess. You've heard about how the young miss has a lot of magic energy, right?"

"Yes, I was informed."

"She has trouble controlling magic because of it. It hasn't happened recently, but in the past the magic she fired would fly in random directions... And each shot had several times more force than that used in actual combat."

That certainly sounded dangerous...

"But like I said, that's in the past. It barely ever happens anymore. Today is more like a precaution."

Camil seemed to be heavily emphasizing that it was okay now. Maybe it was awkward because he was talking about someone he worked for... I felt bad pressing the topic further, so I suggested we get to practicing.

"Good idea. We should begin too. You can use a little bit of attack magic, right?"

"Yes. I can only use the basic attack magics, though."

"Okay. Can you show me all the attack magics you can use?"

"I understand."

I faced a nearby boulder and launched the basic attack magics of the fire, water, wind, earth, lightning, ice, and poison elements — Fireball, Waterball, Windcutter, Earth Needle, Stun, Ice Shot, and Poison, respectively.

"Yup, you've got the basics down well. You'll be able to learn the next magic easy. First... I'll show you an example of each, then you can try for yourself."

"Please do."

"Here I go, then. First is the fire magic, *Fire Arrow*."

The moment Camil chanted the spell, fire converged at his hand to take the shape of an arrow. He threw it straight at the boulder. The arrow hit the target boulder directly, bursting into flames with a light sound.

"First is the elementary attack fire magic, Fire Arrow. It flies faster than Fireball and has more penetration power too. This is the easiest and most popular fire magic to use. Give it a go."

"Okay."

I recalled Camil's Fire Arrow and tried to recreate it. I created enough fire for a Fireball in my hand and compressed it, imagining the shape of an arrow...

"*Fire Arrow.*"

The Fire Arrow I launched was formed just like Camil's magic, flying through the air and bursting upon impact with the boulder.

"Yup, that's a success. You're very quick on the uptake, being able to do it one go."

Huh? In times like this, wasn't the typical reaction in light novels to be suspicious? Should I brush it off?

"I use a bow and arrow, so it was easy to imagine."

"I see, that must have contributed to it."

"Contributed?"

"Yup. It happens sometimes with people who aren't magicians but have high magic-related skill levels. The magic they use in their daily lives gives them the capacity to use attack magic they haven't formally learned yet. With those kinds of people, a little bit of practice and clear imagination allows them to use it. Depending on the person, they can learn it within two or three tries."

Oh, so there was nothing abnormal about learning magic fast... That was good. Come to think of it, the young miss was able to use

Bubbly Water in two tries earlier, too. If I had noticed that, I wouldn't have needed to worry…

After that, we continued in a similar manner until I learned the attack magics *Water Shot*, *Wind Hammer*, *Rock Bullet*, *Stun Arrow*, and *Ice Arrow*. I also learned the defense magics *Fire Wall*, *Water Wall*, *Wind Shield*, and *Ice Shield* in no time at all.

But in return, a little problem occurred.

"Uhh… I've run out of things to teach you… We can move on to intermediate stuff, or work on improving your speed… Hmm…"

It seemed like my magic learning speed wasn't abnormal, but it was still fast, leaving me with nothing else to learn for today. That was when Sebas appeared.

"Is something troubling you?"

"Sebas."

"Ryoma's been so quick on the uptake, he's learned everything for today already."

"I see, so that's what happened. In that case, I can teach him from here. Since I can teach space magic."

Oh, that would be awesome! I could learn space magic from one of the leading magicians in space magic in the kingdom!

"Then my job here is done. Do your best, Ryoma."

"Thank you very much, Camil. I look forward to learning from you, Sebas."

I thanked Camil and bowed my head at Sebas with a merry smile.

"Then let us begin. First, just to confirm, can you use any space magic other than Item Box?"

"I can use Teleport."

"Could you demonstrate it?"

"Yes, of course. *Teleport!*"

Sebas' Side

Master Ryoma activated his Teleport and appeared next to the nearby boulder. He continued to activate it four more consecutive times. After moving around the area, he returned to me.

Due to the nature of teleportation magic spontaneously moving the caster to a different location, it wasn't uncommon to see beginners lose their balance immediately after landing — but I couldn't see any sign of that. Wonderful. It was a basic level of magic, but I could see how experienced he was through his activation speed and natural movements before and after. He seemed to have learned it well, practicing via repetition.

"That was splendid, Master Ryoma. If you can do that much already, I believe you'd be able to use the intermediate magic Dimension Home and mid-range teleportation magic Warp."

"Really?!"

"Yes, really. Master Ryoma, do you know the reason why space magic is categorized as the hardest to use of the higher elements?"

"No, I don't know."

"Then, could you explain how to use space magic?"

"It's built upon the basis of using magic energy to interfere with air and distort it."

"Exactly. However… most people are tripped up by the basic step of using magic energy to interfere with space. Space is something that is always present, but it is rare to find people who are aware of it enough to use it in their magic."

Most textbook examples for space magic had vague wording such as 'engulfing all that is of this world' which left the majority of people with an unclear image within themselves, making their interference incomplete.

All that was required was a comprehensive grasp of where one was located and where the space to use magic was. But this wasn't something that could be explained. Understanding through language was still incomplete. One could only gain a sense of space through repetitive practice. Without that sense, there was no using intermediate or above space magic.

"Many people are shocked by this, but elementary and intermediate space magic are actually the same."

"?!"

Heh... He was as surprised as I expected.

"Long before we were born... there was no elementary space magic, and some even say there was no division of elementary and intermediate magic at all. The reason was because the first step to space magic was to have a proper sense of space. Those who did not have that would fail or have incomplete space magic, but as times changed the number of space magicians decreased and fell in overall quality. Thus, what was formerly basic magic became intermediate magic, and incomplete intermediate magic became elementary magic."

"Does that mean I can use the intermediate Dimension Home and Warp in the same way I use Item Box and Teleport?"

"Yes. Dimension Home will need supplementary explanation, but that is correct for Warp. Extend your teleportation range even further than Teleport, as long as you have a firm grasp of your destination, you can go as far as your magic energy will allow you. Let's see... how about you try the top of that boulder over there, first?"

I pointed to the furthest boulder within visible range. The top of it was flat, so it had the perfect place to stand. It wasn't tall enough to cause great harm from falling, either.

"I'll give it a go."

Master Ryoma immediately took up the challenge. An earnest attitude like that made teaching more worthwhile.

How many magic students have I had now…? Being born with a talent for space magic, in my youth I was zealous about making use of my talent while working for the Jamil house, devoting myself to training and studying as a butler.

When I journeyed with the previous head of the family, that magic proved to be useful. After the journey was over, I assisted the previous head every day… It was from that time on that I was hailed as one of the kingdom's leading space magicians. Being on the move while transporting all of the previous master's belongings in my Dimension Home played a large role in that. I was in the public a lot too.

As a result, many people asked me to take them on as a pupil. I ignored all the written requests addressed to me, but some of them used their connection with the previous head as a shield for me to tutor their sons.

As I couldn't ignore such requests, I taught them… but there wasn't much that could be said for them. I stopped counting the number of students I taught past 100, but ultimately less than ten people were able to reach an intermediate level. There were some noble sons that wouldn't listen when I told them that space magic couldn't be imparted with words and complained instead of practicing.

People like Master Ryoma who listen to what others say earnestly and try to tackle magic practice eagerly — those are the people worth teaching. All the more so if they have the talent. Has there ever been a case where I have voluntarily sought to teach magic? Perhaps so, but I cannot recall.

Even as I'm thinking these things, Master Ryoma has his eyes closed in concentration. Quietly and deeply, as though he cannot hear any of his surroundings. It's wonderful that he has such an impressive concentration for his age, but I wonder what kind of training could result in this...

Looking back on it now, Master Ryoma has been a mystery from the moment we met. I first heard that he was an odd boy with no parents, living alone in the forest. When I actually met him, he was wearing rather clean clothes for a forest lifestyle, and while his speech was awkward, he welcomed us politely. In the house we were invited into, he served high-quality tea and honey. The home was simple, but it was well-built and comfortable to live in — it even had a bathtub. The boy who lived in a house with facilities on par with nobility.

And the oddest of all was his knowledge and abilities. Steadily working away researching slimes that no one else cared about, increasing his quality of life with cleaner slimes and scavenger slimes, even making unheard-of inventions such as waterproof cloth.

On the way to Gimul, he said he could remove the poison from the rock salt in the Forest of Gana with alchemy, then when Master Reinhart expressed interest, he responded with how 'the small quantity would lose to competition from other production areas' — trading knowledge that wasn't available to anyone of his age short of being nobility or receiving merchant education.

His vacant expression when he arrived in the town and his technique in protecting the young miss from crooks was still burned into my mind. And since arriving in town, he's already achieved the tremendous feat of preventing an epidemic before it could spread. None of which would be possible with a normal child. The boy who accomplished it all... Master Ryoma normally seemed mature for his age, but recently he had opened his heart to us more, sometimes showing reactions befitting of his age…

"Sebas."

Oops, I was too immersed in my thoughts…

"Yes, what is it?"

"I think I can do it. I'll give it a go."

"Go ahead."

"…Here goes, *Warp*."

The next moment, Master Ryoma disappeared and appeared on top of the boulder I designated. Once I confirmed that, I teleported as well.

"Congratulations. Your intermediate space magic Warp was a success."

"I did it! Thank you very much, Sebas!"

Fufu… This reaction was most fitting for his age.

"Then let's practice Dimension Home next. Like with Item Box, you open a hole in space and imagine widening it to the size of a large room. I'll leave out that explanation as you can do Item Box already, but when you're creating the space, imagine making an environment identical to what's around you. Unlike Item Box, Dimension Home has air inside. That's why it is possible to keep monsters and sustain life inside. Being unable to recreate this part is what makes Item Box an elementary magic."

"I understand."

After saying that, Master Ryoma began to concentrate. It was a more complex magic than Warp, so Master Ryoma made an effort to grasp a sense of it. He chanted Dimension Home several times, but all that appeared was a black hole. These were all failures. I informed Master Ryoma, and he focused again. And failed again.

Over and over, until he started sweating quite a bit. Despite that, Master Ryoma's focus did not wane.

With the occasional break in between, four hours passed until Master Ryoma muttered, "...*Dimension Home*."

The hole that appeared before Master Ryoma's eyes was... white.

"Congratulations. You've succeeded at Dimension Home as well."

"All right! Thank you very much! Now I can put my slimes inside and move them around!"

"I'm glad to have been of help. If you find the space you've made just now too small, you can make another new space to extend it, though it will use more magic energy. The hole you make will show as black if it's a failure and white if it's a success, so be careful."

"Got it."

"Now, it's about time to return to the young miss. It will be getting dark soon."

"Huh...? Ah! A lot of time has passed..."

It seemed like he hadn't noticed. He may have continued forever if he hadn't succeeded. Any normal person would have depleted their magic energy and thrown in the towel by now... It was clear that he had magic energy that rivaled the young miss in this regard.

"You were concentrating hard, after all. Let's go, then. *Warp*."

There were several intriguing things about him, but I'd continue to watch over him quietly.

～ Chapter 2 Episode 3 ～
Invitation Received

Ryoma's Side

I was focusing so hard I forgot about the time... Sebas brought me back to the present and warped us to where Eliaria and the others were. I only noticed once we arrived, but our Warp practice had moved us pretty far.

"Welcome back, Ryoma."

"Hey. You took quite a while; how far did you go?"

"Did you learn any new magic?"

Once they noticed our arrival, Eliaria's party came running over.

"Yes, thanks to Camil and Sebas."

"That's good. Care to show us, if you still have energy left?"

So Reinbach said. I first went through all the magic I learned from Camil. Next was Dimension Home... It took around ten seconds to open up the entrance. I still needed practice.

"*Dimension Home.*"

It was a success. When the entrance opened, everyone other than Sebas froze. Come to think of it... at my age, using Item Box was impressive enough. I was so excited, I forgot... Oh well. Sebas already knew, so there was no real way of hiding it. In fact, the four of them were already closing in on Sebas.

But they soon came to me to praise me too. I could understand it being an impressive feat, but having my head patted over it was a little embarrassing...

It was nearly sunset after that, so we returned to the inn. However, because steady practice was the best way of learning space magic, I decided to return using Warp. Sebas would accompany me just in case anything happened.

Thus, we were on our way back when Sebas suddenly remembered something.

"Master Ryoma, we are planning on taking Lady Eliaria to the abandoned mine in the mountains for monster combat practice tomorrow. Would you like to join us?"

"That sounds nice. You wouldn't mind if I went too?"

"Of course not, Lady Eliaria would be delighted. Do you possess any weapons other than a bow and arrow? The mines are narrow on the inside, so I do not recommend the use of bows. You will need armor too."

"How about a dagger? I can use magic and martial arts too, but I don't have armor."

"That would suffice as a weapon. The monsters are weak, and the escorts will be there too. The main purpose is to teach my lady how to think about the opponent before moving, and gain that experience."

"Then I shall go with a dagger. As for armor..."

Weapons could be made using earth magic to an extent, but badly made armor would hinder movement.

...Come to think of it, I received a letter of introduction from the guildmaster for this. I should use this chance to buy something proper.

"I think I'll go and buy some once we return to town. I just so happen to have a letter of introduction from the guildmaster of the Adventurer's Guild."

"I see, that's perfect then."

■　■　■

After we reached town, Sebas went back to the inn while I went to search for the armory. When I found the recommended armory and went inside, I was welcomed by a thick-built man with a creepy, wide smile.

"Welcome! Are you after something today?"

"Y-Yes… I'm searching for a weapon I can use in a narrow place, like an abandoned mine. Something like a dagger? And armor as well."

"The daggers are on this shelf; feel free to browse around!"

"…Pardon me for asking, but are you forcing your voice to sound like that?"

"…You can tell?"

"…Very easily so."

His smile had collapsed within seconds, leaving a peculiar expression on his face… When I informed the man of this, he immediately looked surly.

"Argh, enough of that! Sorry, kid. Friend of mine told me I was too gruff, so I tried being friendly. Just wasn't in my nature."

"I see. By the way, this is the Digger Armory, right?"

"Yeah, that's right. Whaddabout it?"

"I received a letter of introduction from the Adventurer's Guild guildmaster. He told me to come here and show you this."

35

"Worgan? Now ain't that odd… You're a newbie, right? We're not a cheap place, though our quality is guaranteed. You have cash?"

"Yes, I don't know the value of weapons, but I can pay up to 30 small golds."

"That's more than enough, then. What didya use until now?"

"I normally use a bow and arrow, but maneuverability inside the mines is a bit…"

"I see… In that case, you can use a dagger like you mentioned, or a short spear or single-handed sword would be good."

"Then I'll take two daggers, and do you have any throwing knives?"

Even though I had a throwing weapon mastery skill, I had only used rocks until now. This was a good chance to stock up.

"It's 1 small gold for 10. They're expensive but good. If you retrieve them afterward and maintain them, they'll last a while."

"Then I'd like to purchase 10 throwing knives and two daggers, please."

"One dagger is 2 small golds, so two and 10 knives makes 5 small golds. And you needed armor too, right?"

"Yes, the easier it is to move around in, the better. What kinds do you have?"

"If you want mobility, it's leather you're after. Monster leather is more sturdy than your run-of-the-mill metal armor, too. There are full-body armors out there that have been enchanted with magic to move as smoothly as leather… but those aren't in circulation here, and we don't stock 'em either."

"Then I shall take the monster leather armor."

"Gotcha. However, I've only got two that would fit your build. If you want something else adjusted, it'll take a day or more. So which will it be? Wanna see them all?"

I had to use it tomorrow, so I needed to buy it today.

"I'm going to the mines tomorrow, so just the armors I can buy today please."

"Aight, then."

The man went around the back and brought out two armors.

"These two are the monster leather armors. One is made from the skin of a grell frog. It's bendy and easy to move in, and is sturdy enough in its own right. It'll cost you 4 medium silvers."

The texture was like rubber. Frogskin, huh…

"The other armor is made from the hard skin of a lizard. This one's pricier and will cost you 5 small golds."

"That's a rather big difference in price."

"It's a matter of materials. The hard lizard lives in the wastelands and is rarely spotted. On top of that, they have an ability similar to the neutral spell Physical Enhancement, so they're quite difficult to hunt. Your average weapons can't cut them, and magic often ends up damaging the skin. I've lowered the price quite a lot already, y'know?"

Physical Enhancement wrapped the skin with magic energy, raising defense and making it harder to wound the body. Monsters that could use it would surely be difficult to hunt.

"To defeat it properly, you need both luck and skill. But the leather's light and can harden if you pass magic energy through it. It enhances durability while keeping the flexibility of the leather, so it's light and easy to move around in. It's even sturdier than regular leather. That's why it's popular among magicians that don't have as much physical energy. However… this one was made from the leftover leather of another armor, so there wasn't enough material to go around. I could only make one the size of a child like you. That's why adult adventurers can't wear it, but at the same time kiddie adventurers like you don't have the coin. I don't have the material

37

to amend the size either. And so, it's remained unsold for two years now. If you have the money, I'd be most grateful if you bought this one. The quality of this one is definitely better."

Indeed, based on his description this one did seem substantially better. The guildmaster personally recommended this store, so he should be trustworthy…

"I understand, I'll take the hard lizard armor."

"Much thanks. Your weapons and armor come to a total of 10 small golds."

I took my coin bag out of my Item Box and paid for the purchase, which the man confirmed before handing me the daggers, knife, and armor to put away.

"Thank you very much. I didn't introduce myself earlier, but I'm Ryoma Takebayashi. I'll be back again if I ever need something."

"Right. I'm the owner, Darson Digger. That armor will last you long if you maintain it well and avoid being reckless. Once you outgrow it, come back to buy another. I'll give you a discount next time."

I thanked him for his words and returned to the inn.

■　　■　　■

The next day.

We set out for the abandoned mines early in the morning, rattling along in the carriage. The path gradually grew bumpier, but the weather was pleasant and we should be arriving soon, since it was roughly three hours' travel from the town…

"…"

I wonder why? Eliaria seemed to be acting strangely. She was sitting beside me, but she hadn't spoken much since breakfast, seemingly deep in thought.

"My Lady, are you all right?"

"Yes, I'm fine."

At least she didn't appear to be sick... Maybe she was nervous?

"Is it possible that you haven't fought with monsters before... and this is your first time?"

"That's not true. I wouldn't say I've had a lot of experience, but..."

"Then you should relax a little, Elia."

"Grandfather..."

"That's right, you won't sound convincing at all if you don't calm down a little."

"Not you too, Mother..."

"Hahaha, it's been a while since the last time, after all. We'll be arriving soon. Shall we go over what we're doing today?"

Figuring it would be more distracting than doing nothing, Reinhart began to speak.

"First, the place we're heading to is called the North Gimul Mine. As its name implies, it's a mine located to the north of Gimul Town, and it's been abandoned already. Now, what is our goal there?"

"To investigate the mines. We need to gather information before we can put out a cleanup request at the Adventurer's Guild. And it'll also be practice for me."

"That's correct. Normally we'd be able to reference the regular patrol reports from the public office, but... after the investigation the other day, we found they'd been dipping their hands into the funds for the northern mines too. The reports won't be as reliable. That's why we'll be going through several mineshafts to gather information on the monsters we see inside, then use that to make a request for the Adventurer's Guild."

It was unclear how many monsters there would be inside the entirety of the north mines, but eliminating them all would be a large job spanning over several days. That's why today was both practice and a simple investigation.

The reports from the public office weren't reliable, but there had been no sightings of high-rank monsters discovered. It would be good practice for a child.

I swayed with the carriage as I looked between the nervous Eliaria and blue sky outside the window.

⇜ **Chapter 2 Episode 4** ⇝
Abandoned Mine Investigation

"Everyone ready?"

""Yes!""

We immediately got to work investigating once we arrived at our destination. Right now, we were in front of the entrance of one of the mineshafts. However, the ground was covered in tall grass, and the exposed rock around the mineshaft was covered in crawling ivy… It must have been a long time since any humans were here.

Eliaria entered the mineshaft with the four usual escorts. The other escorts had come along as well, but they were apparently going to hunt monsters down a different shaft to us.

Furthermore, Reinhart and Elise were going to investigate as a pair, while Reinbach would be on his own.

When I asked if that was all right, Jill answered.

"Don't worry. The three of them used to travel as adventurers. Lord Reinbach has even received medals for his service in the squabbles of neighboring kingdoms. Monsters lurking in an abandoned mine so close to town won't even scratch him."

"They don't actually need us to escort them. The three of them like walking where they want to go and prefer to look after themselves. They have everything they need if Sebas is with them. We didn't follow them into town, yeah?"

"Unlike most high nobility, the young miss's family doesn't like exaggerated formalities. They'll hire brazen fellows like us as long as we're capable of working, and tell us to talk to them normally if we're not in public or before other nobles."

Apparently, the three of them were fairly strong at swords and magic too. I could understand that, but was that really fine? Yeah, I guess it must be.

"We'll do our best too, Ryoma!"

Eliaria usually wore a simple dress made of fabric that even I could tell was high quality, but she was in a shirt and pants today for easier movement. She had what was probably monster leather armor on top of that, and was brimming with motivation.

Did her nerves ease a little?

As we were talking, I noticed Elise waving at us from the entrance of another shaft a distance away. Did Eliaria's voice reach her? After we returned her wave, she gave one more big wave before entering the mineshaft with Reinhart.

Once we saw her off, we also headed inside the mine. Zeph led the way, followed by Jill and Hughes, then Eliaria and I. Camil and my slimes brought up the rear.

We formed a line and walked, but the inside of the shaft was dark. A dozen or so steps in from the entrance and the whole area near the entrance was dark.

"Tch, looks like there aren't any shaft lamps after all."

"Maybe they took them all to use in the east mines?"

"They should have kept them installed until the mine was officially declared abandoned... But based on how it looked outside, the management had been sloppy. If they reused the facilities from here, they'd be able to keep down costs of the east mines for a bit."

"And then they pocketed the extra cash, I see."

"That's the logical conclusion..."

"No matter the truth, it is easy to suspect them. Such is the fate of someone who has betrayed the trust of another. Please be careful, young miss. *Light.*"

Jill wrapped up the conversation and cast a ball of light with basic light magic.

The ball of light hovered above our heads and lit the mineshaft. It didn't reach all the way to the back, but it was enough to see around us.

"Young miss, young master. Please watch where you step. While there won't be any here for obvious reasons, labyrinths and the like can have traps. Spotting them is the role of scouts like me. Today is just a practice, but you must always take care not to step out in front of us."

"Okay!"

"Got it."

We continued walking until something came into view in front of us, at which point Zeph ordered us to stop. I took a closer look, and…

"A bug?"

It was a praying mantis-like bug. However, its body was the same size as me — absurdly large for a mantis. It was no doubt a monster.

…If that was a normal insect instead of a monster, people who hated bugs would find this world hell.

"Do you see it, young master? That's an insect type monster called a cave mantis. It uses its raptorial forelegs to dig holes or find caves and mineshafts to live in."

"Tch! How annoying…"

"Is it strong?"

"It's not strong. Its forelegs aren't exactly sharp and its carapace is soft, so the miners who spot them can beat them up with their pickaxes to eradicate them. But they reproduce fast so there's a high possibility there'll be many of them, including the occasional advanced species, the blade mantis. They look similar to the cave mantis, so it's hard to tell them apart."

"Blade mantises have sharper forelegs than the cave mantis, so if you let your guard down and miss the blade mantis among them you could end up injured. Always take caution."

Jill added to Zeph's warning about the blade mantis. In that case...

"How do you tell them apart?"

"The blade mantis is a little bigger. Though not by much, mind you. The only thing that can help you tell them apart quicker is experience. We just so happen to have a cave mantis over there. I'll pull it over here, so take a close look."

Zeph said, approaching the cave mantis alone, then returning as soon as he was noticed. Then, he blocked the attacks of the cave mantis with a small shield where Elia and I could see.

"That is a cave mantis. Its forelegs can attack at a fairly rapid speed, so watch out."

"Young miss, try defeating it with magic while Zeph's tanking the attacks."

"Don't use fire magic. There's nowhere for the smoke to go inside a cave."

"I understand..."

"Ready anytime, young miss!"

"Then... *Ice Arrow!* Ah! *Ice Arrow!*"

The first Ice Arrow she launched had been evaded, but the second one she sent immediately after that finished the cave mantis off.

"Your magic activation speed is a pass, but you have to take more care with your accuracy."

"I understand..."

After that, we walked for another two minutes to find more cave mantises. This time there were four.

"What should we do... I was thinking of letting Ryoma have a turn, but is four too many at once?"

Since that was directed at me, I answered that I'd try.

"Be careful."

I nodded and drew the two daggers at my waist, activating the neutral magic Physical Hardening. When I ran at the cave mantis, one of them turned my way and raised its right foreleg.

Before it could swing it down, I used my left leg to kick the right foreleg supporting the cave mantis's balance and broke it. The cave mantis lost its balance and collapsed. I crushed its head under my feet and turned to the second one approaching.

The second mantis had swung its left foreleg up, so I waited for the right timing when it swung down to turn my body 90 degrees. Avoiding its attack by a hair's breadth, I used my right dagger to slice through its joints, then my left dagger to send its head flying as I turned my body back.

Behind it was the third one. I adjusted my left dagger from an underhand grip to an overhand one, spinning my body anti-clockwise. Evading with my right arm, I closed in. Then dropped its head with my left arm.

"Kyah!"

The fourth one cried out, swiping its left foreleg out horizontally. It was aimed at my head, but I was moving closer so it missed. All that was left was to parry with my right dagger, then cut off its limbs with my left. Next came the right foreleg. In the same way, I blocked with my left arm and cut it off with my right. The cave mantis had no way of resisting once it lost both its forelegs, making it easy to behead.

…There was no particular problem. There wasn't even a scratch on my daggers.

I confirmed that they had been finished off completely before returning.

"Good work. Looks like you have no trouble with close combat. Young miss, insect type monsters can be tenacious, so never let your guard down unless you've twisted its neck or trampled its head like Ryoma."

"I understand."

"It was a good choice to guard yourself with hardening magic. A cave mantis's attacks would be no problem at all with a hardened body."

"That's amazing, Ryoma."

I was used to insect type monsters from the green caterpillars in the Forest of Gana, after all. They were weak monsters that had a lot of vitality. Having to catch them for slime food meant that I grew unwittingly used to them.

Once we had finished our first battles, we continued down the mineshaft path. Ten minutes later, I was walking in the lead with Eliaria behind me, fighting the monsters we encountered.

The only monster in our way was the cave mantis. Rather than practice, it was more like a monotonous pest extermination, so Jill and the other agreed it wouldn't be a problem for me to do so, but… the more we progressed, the more the number of cave mantises increased. On top of there being four to five of them at once, there was a shorter interval between them. This wasn't a big deal for me.

"Oof."

Cave mantises were really weak.

But it was a different matter for the young miss. With her ice magic, she could aim at enemies in the distance and weaken them, lowering their numbers. While it was helpful for me to have support, the continuous battles were a strain on her stamina. The amount of magic energy she used each time was gradually increasing.

I'm sure the four at the back would protect her if it came to it, but...

"*Playing Clay!*"

"?!"

The foot the mantis stepped out with suddenly sunk, knocking it off balance and making it easy to finish off.

"How about a break?" I suggested.

"Here's some jerky. Eating a little will help you feel better."

"Thank you very much."

The break was accepted easily.

We were still wary of the depths of the mineshaft that could contain unseen monsters, but we sat down to rest ourselves. It was bright enough with the Light spell, and there was air ventilation coming from somewhere too. That's why it didn't feel suffocating at all. It was a little humid, but it was good enough to rest in.

"Are you okay, Miss?"

"Thank you for thinking about me. My physical and magical energy are still fine. But I do feel like I'm getting more tired than usual."

"It's a common thing, being more tired fighting in a place you're not familiar with. Especially in places like this, where you can't tell that time's passing. There's nothing you can do but get used to it — that's what practice is for. How are you holding up by the way, Ryoma?"

Camil gave his advice before turning to me, but it was already a familiar environment to me.

"My house felt like this, so."

"Ah, that's right, I remember."

Camil nodded in understanding, which seemed to make Hughes recall something.

"Come to think of it, Ryoma. What was the spell you used on the cave mantis that made it trip earlier? I could tell it was earth magic, but…"

"Playing Clay? It's a magic that temporarily turns dirt and stone into clay."

It was a spell that used the same combination as Create Rock, which I used during the landslide: Break Rock to break down dirt, and Rock to keep the particles connected. And it was also the magic he created to play around when he still couldn't use magic well. He'd given it the name Playing Clay for that reason.

"Back then, I found it difficult to make the shape I wanted in one use of Rock, so I shaped most things by hand. I'd hold the rock in my hand like so, then pour magic energy into it and knead it into clay. Eventually I grew more experienced and got better at using Rock too."

Also, the material would return to its original form after the flow of magic energy ran out. Dirt would return to dirt, and stone would return to stone.

That's what made it a convenient magic to use when filling in cracks in the walls and repainting them. Though I wasn't thinking that far when I first created it.

While I was talking, five sets of eyes including Eliaria's were looking at me in exasperation.

"Hey, Camil, Jill. What do you think? You guys are in charge of magic."

"Creating a new magic just because you can't do a certain basic magic well... Ryoma's actions never cease to surpass expectations..."

"I won't say it's impossible, but it's certainly tiresome. It would be one thing to be taught it, but creating magic yourself takes more effort than simply practicing hard at it."

They discussed the topic as I rested at ease. For the record, my slimes had been eating the monsters we had defeated this entire time. It was plain work, but they were extremely useful in clearing the path.

⤳ **Chapter 2 Episode 5** ⤳
True Alchemy

"Ah… Nothing like fresh air."

The monster extermination of the first mineshaft was over without incident, and Hughes smiled in comfort once we were back outside.

"There's no time to enjoy the air; we have to go back and make a report."

"I know, I know. But it'll be just in time for lunch after that. Another break, yay."

They called out to us, and we all headed for the entrance of the mines together.

There was a square there used for the transport of ores and mining tools in and out of the mine, so unlike other boulder-ridden places, this one was flattened neatly. Today, the carriage was parked there as our gathering point, but apparently there used to be an employee breakroom back when the mine was still open.

"Ooh!"

We parted our way through wild waist-high grass, walking up hills and along rocky areas with the wind occasionally blowing strongly. One side of the road was a cliff, so that probably played a part. With no shielding, the wind warmed by the sun's rays felt like freedom and comfort.

When I glanced in the direction the wind was blowing, I could see the road we used on our way from Gimul Town before me. Under the clear blue sky without a single cloud, the straight road extending through the overgrown greenery was tranquil to see.

"Young master. Please be careful. The cliff is that way."

"Thank you very much."

Zeph gave me a warning. Getting too close would certainly be dangerous. It was hard to see my feet with all the grass too…

When I looked down, I saw large amounts of dirt and gravel roughly piled below the cliff. Was that what they called a spoil tip — a mountain made from the dirt that came out of a mine? I had never seen one with my own eyes before.

It couldn't be called pretty, but the red dirt with weeds sprouting out in patches gave a feeling of nature's vitality. However…

"Such a shame…"

They said the iron output of this mine was already zero, but what if it was just the ores that were gone while the iron content in the soil remained? That red dirt was the color of iron oxide — the color of rust, right? I could probably turn it to iron with alchemy… But I guess that wouldn't work if alchemy was seen as a shady act run by scammers.

As I was thinking such things, we arrived at the gathering point. For some reason, Reinhart and Elise were waiting at the entrance.

"Welcome back!"

"How did it go?"

"Mother, Father, I defeated lots of cave mantises!"

"Hmm, seems like it went well."

"Ryoma blocked them from getting close to me, so I was able to use my magic with ease. He defeated even more than I did!"

"You protected her, Ryoma? Thank you."

"But… were there really that many cave mantises?"

"It seemed like the mineshaft we went into was a cave mantis nest. There wasn't a single other monster."

"I see, then how about you take a different mineshaft after lunch? Would you like to go with us this time? I want to see Elia and Ryoma fight too."

"Really? I'll do my best!"

"My, my. But first, it's time for lunch. The others should be back soon too. Tell me the details about the first shaft while we wait."

Thus, we gave our detailed report and had lunch. The second shaft was to wait until afterward.

■　■　■

"Speaking of which, Ryoma. What were you thinking about earlier?"

"Earlier?"

During lunch with the four members of the Jamil family. We were chatting away normally about our thoughts of the morning and Elia's fighting style when she changed the topic and asked me that question. But I had no idea what she was talking about.

"You were looking at the scenery and saying it was a shame earlier."

Oh, back then. I understood now, but it was a little difficult to answer.

"N-No, it was nothing."

Ah, that wasn't convincing at all.

Even I could tell my words were far from the truth.

"How suspicious. Very suspicious."

"You're not good at lying, are you?"

"Is it something you can't say?"

"You can say whatever you want without holding back, you know?"

I guess I didn't mind telling these people…

"Do you remember what I talked about in the carriage on the way to Gimul Town? Umm… about the salt."

"Ah… I see. It's fine, it's just us, Sebas, Araune, and Lilian here. Araune and Lilian won't breathe a word either."

"I see. Then I'll tell you. You know how I can use alchemy?"

"So you've said."

Reinhart was the one who answered me, but my attention was on Araune and Lilian. The two of them reacted in slight surprise at the mention of alchemy, but I couldn't see any disgust. I continued in relief.

"Right, so this mine is about to become abandoned, right?"

"Indeed. The procedure for it is all completed."

"Is something the matter with that?"

"I think you can still harvest iron from it. If you use alchemy."

My words made everyone stiffen this time.

"Is that… true?"

"Yes. I told you about how I took the poison out of the salt in the Forest of Gana, right?"

"You did."

"Iron can be removed from the discarded dirt in the same way. The color of the red dirt is probably iron rust… Umm, you know if you leave your sword in water, it'll rust?"

"Of course."

"The iron in the dirt reacts in the same way, turning into that color. So if you break it down once or twice with alchemy, you should be able to extract only the iron. But if large amounts of iron started appearing from an abandoned mine, it'd be strange, right?

There's also the issue of alchemy itself… which is why I found it such a shame."

"That's certainly true, but… Ryoma, if you think you can do it, could you give it a go? I'm very curious about what you've said, and there are legal ways to sell it without causing a fuss."

"Sure."

I agreed readily.

I wasn't fussed about keeping my alchemy a secret in front of people who didn't find it a problem. After all, Gain threw together the process at the request of an otherworlder, so it was very simple. A school level knowledge of science and the elements was enough to use it. The reason why alchemy hadn't spread in this world was because of the prejudice and lack of that knowledge.

But to be honest, when it came to extracting just the iron…

What was iron oxide? Iron that had oxidized.

What did 'oxidize' mean? The combination of matter and oxygen. In the case of iron oxide, it was the combination of iron and oxygen.

What was oxygen? Part of the air we were breathing at this very moment.

What should be done through alchemy? Separate the combined oxygen and iron using magic energy, returning it to iron (deoxidation).

…If I told them this right now, Reinhart and Eliaria would probably be able to do it too.

If that wasn't enough, I could explain more details about oxygen. That much information would take less than an hour to explain. Though I had no intention of teaching them in detail if I wasn't asked.

If they wanted to use it for business or personal reasons, they were free to do so. Even if it was created by the whims of an otherworlder, it was still a legitimate skill in this world.

Then, after lunch.

"Ryoma, will this do?"

"Yes, thank you very much."

I drew the magic circle needed for alchemy on the ground (a square inside a circle) and placed the containers of red dirt prepared for me on top.

"I'm going to begin. It's dangerous, so make sure you do not step on the circle."

With that warning, I pushed magic energy through the circle to watch it glow with a curtain of light. The spectators watched without making a sound, staring in deep interest.

I was like that at first too... But the sensation was now like turning on my PC... Actually, I might be even more excited to turn on a PC right now. Because of the memories. Oops, I should stop getting distracted and get to work...

There were different magic circles for different alchemy purposes, and the one I was using now was the separation circle. If I willed for only the iron oxide to be separated from the dirt, the dirt would float up and outside of the circle by itself. At this point, the only thing that could pass the curtain of light was dirt, and when the light disappeared the reddish-brown particles remained inside the containers. Using the neutral magic Appraisal showed it was indeed iron oxide.

I separated this once more, taking the oxygen from the iron oxide. This left sparkling silver grains. In this state, it would blow away with the wind… I drew the circle for combination, a circle and five-pointed star, next to the separation circle.

It required the user's imagination and knowledge of what the original substance and combined substance was to be, but using this circle allowed the materials on top to be combined. So, if I used this to make it into one lump… Done.

I appraised the completed lump for a final check, and it was indeed 100% pure iron. There was no mistaking it.

…Yeah, the fact I thought that way was proof I had become used to alchemy, even though I had been so excited about the unbelievable phenomenon at first. Having people to compare myself with in front of me made me realize that all the further.

"Reinhart, it's a success. Please confirm for yourself."

I handed the lump over to Reinhart who was staring intently at my hands and he proceeded to touch it and hit it, turning it over and holding it up to the light before casting his own appraisal magic.

"Iron, yup. It's iron, all right. You actually made iron… I'm sorry, Ryoma."

"Huh?! Why are you apologizing?! Please raise your head!"

I faltered at the sudden apology. What happened in such a short time?

Reinhart raised his head, but still looked regretful as he opened his mouth.

"That's, well… It's a common scam that alchemy can be used to make money. I didn't believe you would scam people, but I didn't think you could make iron either. I doubted your words."

Oh, so that's what it was.

"So asking you to show me while doubting you was…"

"If it's similar to the methods of scammers, I don't blame you for doubting it. There was no harm done, so it's fine."

"I'm grateful you see it that way. But still… true alchemy is amazing. To think iron could be made from that dirt."

"And this iron is very clean. It's almost like silver."

"That's true. Is it because it's made from alchemy?"

"Unfortunately, this can't be sold as it is. While it definitely is real iron and Master Ryoma's alchemy was wonderful…"

Rather than it being an issue of alchemy, the purity was the problem. This was a lump of pure iron made by gathering iron particles and hardening it with magic. Super high purity iron had a shine to it, was soft and malleable, and rusted less than normal iron.

…Or so I think I heard on TV once. I never imagined I'd be making it myself. In fact, the news hadn't introduced any super high 100% purity iron, so maybe that was the magic. If I was to use the common sense from my previous life, separation via magic was already weird.

Well, that aside… knowing the problem meant a solution could be considered. If the purity was too high, would it be fine if I just dropped it?

I drew a six-pointed star in a circle and placed the dirt removed earlier on top of it.

The purpose of the six-pointed star circle was mixing, allowing for multiple types of substances to be mixed without bias. It wasn't an as often used circle, but if it was just to drop the purity… I thought as I watched the color fade to a dark-ish color. It eventually reached the color of a regular iron product, but that didn't mean it was one. There were differences in the impurities in the iron, such as iron with more carbon being harder but more brittle.

That was why I didn't know if it could be used as regular iron. When I told Reinhart that, he laughed and said this.

"In that case, I know of trustworthy merchants who can look into that for you. If you'd like, I can introduce them to you."

"Really? I would love that."

"Of course. Let's see, who would be good... Or maybe even a blacksmith instead?"

Since I had made it, I was curious about its quality. Which is why I requested the favor, but...

After that, Reinhart became so focused on deciding who to talk with, he didn't participate in the afternoon monster exterminations.

Eliaria was a little upset about that, puffing up her cheeks... What should I do?

❧ Chapter 2 Episode 6 ❧
Afternoon Expedition and a Gift

With Reinhart sitting out of the afternoon expedition, it was decided that I, Eliaria, Elise, and Reinbach would operate together.

"Honestly, Father's always like that when it comes to work…"

"He shouldn't be neglecting you and his own daughter. Don't you agree?"

"Since I was one of the reasons for it, I have no right to speak… and Reinhart is just passionate about his work. It's better than being lazy."

"That's true… We've arrived; it's here."

The two adults had led us to the entrance of a large mineshaft.

"Now from here onwards, the two of you will be making the main decisions. Father-in-law and I will follow you. We'll step in if you're in danger, but we won't assist otherwise."

"This is mainly an activity for Elia to gain experience, as Ryoma already has a lot. Sorry for asking this, Ryoma, but could you refrain from taking the lead too much yourself as well?"

Eliaria was suddenly given a mission.

"I'll do my best."

"I understand."

Seeing the young lady accept the task without hesitation made me realize she was used to being given surprise missions from these two. When she boldly stepped inside the mineshaft, we could see that the shaft this time was wider and the walls were covered in moss here and there. It looked like it could be easy to slip on. We should be careful.

"It's so dark, I can't see very far."

The thought had crossed my mind in the morning, but unlike me, who was used to hunting in the darkness of the night, it seemed like Eliaria didn't have much visibility.

"Ryoma, what do you do when you're hunting at night? Do you use light magic?"

"In the cases that I don't mind my approach being noticed, yes. But when I'm attacking bandits or acting stealthily, I use the neutral magic Probe. There's a risk of having the magic energy detected, but it's less obvious than Light."

"I can't use Probe very well. How do you do it? I learned that it was like widening your awareness, but I don't understand it well."

Probe was... let's see... After thinking for a moment, I used earth magic to create a bowl and filled it with water magic.

"Look at this."

"Hm?"

I showed her the bowl and dropped a pebble into the center, which naturally created ripples along the surface.

"The pebble in the middle is you, and the ripples are the flow of your magic energy. Using yourself as the center, spread your magic energy out as waves and search for any monsters."

I dropped in several more small pebbles, suppressed the waves with magic, then dropped another stone in the center. Ripples traveled across the surface once more, but this time they were hindered by the small pebbles.

"Your magic energy will be interrupted by monsters in this way. If you think of it as the probe catching monsters and people in this way, then..."

"I see, that's a better explanation than before. Umm... *Probe!*"

The moment Eliaria activated the Probe magic, a rather large amount of magic energy scattered from her. An amount so large, I had only ever felt that much from myself before.

Even if I didn't concentrate, I could feel it. It was, to put it simply, amazing. But if there was ever an enemy magician, they'd probably notice it immediately...

Being able to feel the magic energy within yourself was the most basic of the basics for magic. In other words, no matter one's specialty, there were no magicians that couldn't detect magic.

"There are many a little further ahead."

"Then it's a success. But, you used a little too much magic energy. If there was a magician here, you would have definitely been discovered."

"R-Really? I'll need to practice more."

"I'll take care of the front line and using Probe. You should focus on your magic just like in the morning."

"All right. In that case, I'm counting on you, Ryoma."

Leave it to me. Since she said there was something in front of us, I also used Probe to confirm that there was a large number of monsters. However, it seemed like a gathering of rather small individual bodies.

"The road widens to a large cave in front of us, and it seems like there's something covering the ceiling there. If they're on the ceiling, are they cave bats?"

"The ceiling should mean they're cave bats. But if they're covering the entire ceiling, wouldn't that be a bit tough for Elia?"

"If it were just one or two it would be good accuracy practice, but a swarm means firing anywhere would make contact."

Cave bats were bat monsters that mostly fed off insects, and were around the size of an adult hand. They were basically the same as Earth bats. They barely had any form of attack, and they were weak enough for even a child to defeat, but they were fast and flew around so they were hard to hit. As monsters, they were ranked F, which made them quite annoying when they swarmed together. The two adults didn't look that enthusiastic about it either.

"How about an experiment, then?"

""""Experiment?"""

"Yes. If it goes well, we might be able to take out all the cave bats at once."

I first confirmed that the cave bats were pretty much the same as Earth bats once more. Which was why my suggestion was to use sound. If we used magic to fire a loud sound at the cave bats, wouldn't they all be knocked out at once?

After all, there were non-lethal weapons like stun grenades in my previous world, and sound could be removed by suppressing the vibrations in the air with Silent. Contrarily, vibrations could be amplified to make sounds louder with Big Voice. There were also things like Voice Change, which altered a voice to resemble the effects of breathing helium, Whisper, which could send sound as far as the eye could see, and Sound Bomb, which combined the effects of Big Voice and Whisper. These and many more were all sound-related magics I researched while I was in the forest, which should make things work out.

Especially Sound Bomb, which burst a black bear's eardrums and knocked it out during one of my experiments. My only worry was that the sound magic Whisper required practice where I stood in a room alone continuously mumbling to myself, which made me feel so lonely that I stopped using it over a year ago... If the magic didn't fail, it should have an effect on the bats.

The other three issues were whether the mineshaft would collapse from the loud sound, whether there were other people in the vicinity, and what to do if the cave bats weren't finished off.

"There's no need to worry about the mineshaft. The shaft has been secured with earth magic to prevent cave-ins, so there's very little chance of that happening. I've confirmed the lack of people with Probe, and if you can't finish them off..."

"...Shall I rely on the slimes?"

"Indeed. If that doesn't work, we'll assist."

With that decided, I took a big sticky slime out of my Dimension Home.

"Work hard, you guys."

I ordered it to maximize itself to block the mineshaft then approach the cave bats slowly, making its body into a mesh net. Once it followed those instructions, a sticky net was set up before us. Finally, I used barrier magic to surround everything past the slime net to the depths of the cavern, putting up a soundproof barrier to prevent sound from leaking out.

"It's ready."

"You can go ahead whenever."

"Then, *Sound Bomb*."

The next moment, a tremendous explosive sound probably echoed within the mineshaft. Even if we couldn't hear it, we could see the shadows dropping from the ceiling.

"It looks like it worked. Let's go."

After undoing the barrier, we pressed forward with the slime net as a shield to find a mountain of cave bats had fallen on the floor of the mineshaft. Most of them were knocked out and unable to flee, there were just barely ten bats left flying. Those that remained fluttered unsteadily into the walls and fell. Some of the cave bats made it to us, but they were entangled in the sticky slime's net.

"Oh my, this is…"

"He really defeated them in one spell."

"That's amazing, Ryoma!"

"It's been a while since I used it, but I'm glad it worked. Looks like the sharp ears of the cave bats became their downfall. Ah, can I feed them to my slimes?"

"You're the one who finished them, so you can do as you please."

"There's nothing profitable from cave bats anyway."

I ordered the big sticky slime to separate and let the 364 individual sticky slimes eat all the cave bats.

Oh, some of the sticky slimes were ready to split again. I'd have to let them split once we returned to the inn…

After that, the slimes and I continued to support Eliaria in hunting the remaining monsters in the mineshaft for the next hour.

■　■　■

"Hey, Ryoma!"

We came out of the second mineshaft to find Reinhart was waiting for us at the entrance.

"Did something happen?"

"It's about the iron. I was hoping you could make a lump of iron to show the store owner as a sample. Preferably in the shape of a long ingot, if possible."

"I can do that. If I use the alchemy circle for transformation, it will only take a moment."

"Really? Then I'd like to ask for it right away."

And so, Reinhart and I swapped spots as I went about making the ingot. Reinhart offered to help, but I could do it alone so I sent him off with Eliaria. The work wasn't so difficult that I needed help, so he should treat his family with his presence instead.

As proof my thoughts weren't wrong, the ingot was done in no time at all. The time it took to move to the spoil tip was the same time it took to work.

"Sebas, I'm done with the ingot."

"Indeed, I shall hold onto this... What will you do now, Master Ryoma?"

"Let's see..."

I was thinking of returning to the monster extermination, but the others were already inside the mines.

Should I go into a mineshaft by myself? But the monsters here were honestly too weak to put up a fight, and considering the amount of time left until we had to go back to town... Not to mention, today's goal was investigation. The overall subjugation would be done by hiring adventurers from the town, so there was no need to rush... I should take this time to increase my slimes.

"My slimes are about to split, so I think I'll work on forming contracts and training."

"In that case, please use the square. The space is free, and I'll be within range if you need anything."

Thus, I let my slimes split and spent the rest of the time practicing leisurely.

One hour later.

Eliaria and the others returned to a square that was occupied by slimes split by type.

"Ryoma!"

"Ah, my lady. Have you finished your training?"

"Yes, I'm done for today. I have a present for you."

"A present?"

"Heh heh… I think you'll like it a lot."

Eliaria and Elise said, as Reinhart handed me a stone box.

"There's a monster inside. It's weak, but be careful when you open it."

Reinbach warned me accordingly, so I warily opened the lid. The next moment, my breath was taken away by the monster inside the box.

"A slime?"

Inside was a dark gray slime I had never seen before, squirming as it searched for the exit.

"It's a metal slime, one of the many advanced species of slimes out there. We came across it by coincidence and caught it."

"Can I really have it? Thank you very much! I'm so happy! Another new species of slime…"

"A slime is still a monster, so you'd better make a contract with it first."

Oops, that was right.

I snapped back to my senses at Reinbach's words and conducted the taming contract. The metal slime settled down inside the box, so I picked it up and found it really was of a metallic texture. It was also heavier than the other slimes I've had. If this was a metal slime, then its diet must be metal.

"Oh right, Reinhart. Can I take some of the dirt with iron particles in it to feed this slime?"

"You're going to feed it dirt?"

"Either the dirt, or I'll take out the iron and feed it. Also some to experiment on the other slimes."

"In that case, you can take as much as you want. It was originally thrown out as mining waste. If you hadn't mentioned it, we wouldn't have even looked at it."

"Thank you very much!"

If I piled it all up in a corner of the dimension home, I should have enough for a while. If I fed a slime metal... Would it turn into a metal slime? Or would it turn into a different slime... I looked forward to seeing the results.

"By the way, Ryoma, what are you doing?"

"Oh, I'm increasing my slimes and practicing a little combat..."

"Combat... with slimes?"

Eliaria didn't look convinced. Well, I could get what she meant. Even if the things I had told her until now helped her understand that slimes were convenient, she still didn't know much about their combat. From society's point of view, slimes were G-rank monsters that could be defeated by children. And in reality, they *were* weak.

However, their soft half-liquid bodies and immortality when their cores were protected were very useful characteristics.

Slimes were also able to move their cores anywhere in their body, so they could protect their core while being kicked by moving it to the opposite side, then absorb the shock with their half-liquid body. If they were blown away, they could similarly avoid damage during the landing. These were all possibilities I had once considered.

Wild slimes were sluggish so I had assumed it was impossible, but ever since I noticed the slimes I had spent a long time with were more keen and nimble, I had been training with them in the forest.

Techniques to slip past an opponent swinging their weapon down in a one-on-one battle, avoiding the weapon and entangling the arm that drew closer with the approach. Making use of their half-liquid body to evade a weapon or attack, increasing their evasion and defense — that was what I focused on teaching them. However, the current result was slimes with parts of their bodies stretched to hold spears or staffs.

"That being said, they still can't take on a goblin in one-on-one battle, and generally just lack power."

"No no no, a slime holding a weapon is amazing already!"

"Ryoma, how about you take a beginner lesson at the Tamer's Guild? You'll learn a lot of general knowledge."

"If anything, they should be the ones asking Ryoma to hold the lessons..."

I had faintly realized it already, but my slimes were really looked down on.

The three of them suddenly had tired looks on their faces, but I asked them for assistance and Eliaria helped me move the red dirt from the spoil tip.

We spent the rest of the time doing that, and by the time we departed from the mines there was a mountain of red dirt blocks stacked in a corner of my Dimension Home.

⇌ Chapter 2 Episode 7 ⇌
Morgan Trading Company

"You look a little tired, Ryoma. Is everything okay?"

On the way back from the mines, Reinhart said that to me.

"I was thinking of dropping by some people who would cooperate with the sales of your iron, slime string, and the waterproof fabric you designed, but…"

"I'm fine. I just used a little too much magic energy."

I had used Create Block to turn a large amount of red dirt into bricks, so I was feeling a little close to running out of magic energy but otherwise fine. It wasn't as though I had run out of energy, and this much exhaustion wouldn't impact my work.

About an hour after Reinhart asked that, the carriage arrived in town, stopping before a certain merchant's store. There was nothing flashy about the store's appearance, but the store and its surroundings were constructed as large wooden buildings that gave an air of cleanliness. I figured it must be a high-class store for the duke and his family to visit, but the store wasn't intimidating, in a good way.

When we entered the store, we were immediately led to the large reception room at the back. The wall here was decorated with paintings, and decorative vases sat in the corner. It was a room with far much more expensive tastes than the exterior. I sat on the sofa as prompted, but it was so soft I sunk into it.

...It was a little more extravagant than the reception rooms I remembered from my past life, so I felt a little out of place... I should just stay quiet beside Sebas.

I sat just meekly enough not to seem pathetic and waited until, eventually, a well-built man appeared. He was probably the owner of this store.

"My, oh my, the entire ducal family has come to visit together."

"Long time no see, Serge."

"It's good to see you again. You and your family treat me well on a daily basis, yet the chance to meet face-to-face is so rare. I'm glad to see everyone looks healthy too. I believe this person is a new face. My name is Serge Morgan, president of the Morgan Trading Company."

Oh, he greeted me as well.

"I'm Ryoma Takebayashi. Various circumstances have placed me under the care of the Jamil family. It's nice to meet you."

I returned the greeting with a smile. I was told that I could trust him, but I wondered what kind of person he was...

"Now, to get straight to business..."

"Did you bring something new again today?"

The two began their business discussions as I was thinking. Since he said 'again,' Reinhart must bring products here fairly often.

"Before I show you the product, I'd like you to promise me something. You must not leak information about what you're about to see anywhere. I trust you, Serge, but just in case."

"Why, of course. Information about our business partners is the most valuable thing to us. If you don't want anything leaked, we will take all the extra precautions to make sure it remains secret. However, I must say it's not something I've heard you request before, Lord Reinhart."

71

"There are some circumstances… but I'm certain the profits this time will be on another level."

Was it really that amazing? I guess raincoats were everyday items in my previous life… my sense of the standard might be off…

"Sebas."

At Reinhart's command, Sebas took the waterproof fabric, slime thread, and iron ingot I made out from his Item Box.

"This cloth has been processed in a particular way."

"May I pick it up?"

"Of course."

Serge expressed interest in the fabric as soon as he held it, inspecting the waterproof surface closely.

"Hmm, it's nice to the touch."

"That's not all that's nice about it. That fabric can repel water without letting it soak to the other side."

"…Really?"

"You can look it up with Appraisal, or actually wrap it around your hand and dip it in water. I brought that here as a sample."

"Then, if you don't mind me…"

Serge called a servant to prepare a bowl of water, then used Appraisal while he was waiting. His eyes sparkled as he read the information, and as soon as the servant brought the water over, he wrapped his hand in it and stuck it into the water to test its repellency.

"Lord Reinhart, this is a fabulous item!"

"Right? Don't you think this fabric would sell well as rain protection?"

"It'll sell! This will most definitely sell!"

He was really into it!

"And that's not all. Next is this string."

"Allow me to see."

This time he picked up the thread and inspected it, touching it and pulling it. Then he said one sentence.

"Could this possibly be processed with the same material as the fabric?"

He noticed?! No one gave him any hint, yet he could tell just by touching it?

Hearing Serge's response made Reinhart nod with a smile.

"I knew you'd see it, Serge. That's correct. The process is a little different, but the same material is being used. Well? Doesn't it make a fine thread?"

"Indeed, high end tailors would swarm to purchase this. The beauty of the thread is a factor, but it's sturdy as well."

"This is clothing made from that fabric and thread."

As he said that, he took out the work overalls and long boots I made… Huh? I already had my work outfit with me. Did he make new ones? When did he have the time?

"These are work clothes for use in wet and dirty places. The design is a little eccentric, but its functionality is superb."

"Indeed, I believe there will be laborers who would want this. If we can convey the benefits to the people, they could explode in popularity."

"You'd need something to trigger that explosion, but there's a high possibility there. And finally, there's this."

Reinhart moved the work overalls and long boots to the side to take out the iron ingot last.

"May I appraise it?"

"Of course."

Serge appraised it before turning to Reinhart with a slightly disappointed slump in his shoulders.

"It's a fine item, but… to be honest, it looks like your average iron ingot to me."

"Then take a look at this ingot instead."

Sebas took out the other ingot (of the highest iron purity) and passed it to Serge.

"Is this aluminum? But this weight is… Allow me to inspect it."

The moment he said that and used Appraisal, his jaw dropped at the results. He tried to pull himself together, but he was sweating profusely in clear discomposure.

"Lord Reinhart, this ingot is…"

"Amazing, right? Don't you think riots would start if this was sold?"

"Naturally so. This sheen that could be mistaken for silver… It would be clear to anyone that it is unlike any pre-existing item. Some would even try to pry into its production."

"And that's what the ingot from earlier is for. That one had been modified from an ingot like the one in your hands to make it similar to existing ingots."

Serge nodded in understanding.

"I understand the circumstances, but that would make it nothing more than regular iron. It won't gather much attention; will that be okay?"

"That would be fine. We wish to sell this ingot lawfully but with secrecy. This ingot was sourced from the mines, but it isn't as though new veins were discovered."

"I see. So you wish to include that and keep its production a secret while selling the completed ingots, is that correct?"

"Exactly. To be more precise, I'd like it to be exported to other kingdoms. Selling it within the kingdom would require stating its place of origin, but exports only need to state the kingdom, yes?"

"Yes. That won't be an issue."

That was all that was needed for an all-clear?! Really?!

"Also, bringing the ingots here also serves to keep the creator's identity a secret. I'm asking this of you because I trust you, Serge."

"Thank you kindly."

"Now, as for the creator... These three items were all developed by the same person."

Oh, that's not the point you should be surprised about. I was about to be introduced.

"These three wonderful items were all made by the same person?"

Reinhart grinned at Serge's response and said, "That's right. The one who created these was Ryoma over here."

The moment those words left Reinhart's lips, Serge was stunned into looking between Reinhart and I with wide eyes.

"What did you just say...?"

"Ryoma over here was the inventor of these items. It may be hard to believe, but it's the truth."

"Did you really make these things, Master Takebayashi?"

"Yes, I did."

"It's true. I'd like you to keep this a secret... But despite his young age, Ryoma is both an excellent researcher and alchemist."

Serge's expression seemed to look a little dubious the moment he heard the word alchemist... I guess alchemists were really untrustworthy...

"I understand your doubts, but he created this ingot before my very own eyes. He isn't a scammer."

"In front of Lord Reinhart's very own eyes... Could I ask to witness the process as well?"

Oh, despite his suspicions, he was willing to confirm the truth before brushing me aside. Well, I was brought here by the duke

76

himself... I didn't have much magical energy left, but I'd have to do what I could.

"I've used a little too much magical energy today, so would something small suffice?"

"In that case, my store has magic replenishing potions in stock, so feel free to use them. Since this is at my request, it's the least I can offer."

Huh, really? I could have them? Then there shouldn't be an issue.

"Then, could I have two sheets of paper and a writing utensil along with the potion? I need them for the magic circle."

Serge called his servant once again to retrieve the potion, pen and paper.

"Will this do?"

"That's perfect. Thank you."

I thanked him and drew two simple magic circles on the papers before taking 5 bricks of red dirt out of my Item Box.

"This is dirt from the mines, hardened by earth magic. It will act as the base material, so please check for yourself."

Serge immediately used Appraisal on it.

"Indeed, that is what it is."

"Now, please make sure you don't place any body parts into the magic circle while I work. It's very dangerous. I shall begin now."

I passed magic energy through the circles and watched them light up, quickly making an iron ingot before handing it over.

"Please inspect it."

Serge, whose eyes had been as round as plates the whole time I worked, accepted the ingot and appraised it. The next moment, he leaped up from the sofa.

"Please accept my deepest apologies!"

He bowed deeply with respectful elegance.

"No, no, not at all! Please raise your head, there's no need for this. I know people can be wary of alchemists, so your reaction was better than the average person already!"

Despite having the Jamil family's support, I was still a child. Being apologized to so sincerely by someone above me just didn't feel right.

If he had brushed me off or expressed his suspicions through negative words and actions, I would have been able to treat him like my previous boss in a business relationship...

"I'm grateful for your words. I didn't expect a true alchemist to be here... May I ask if you're actually an older age than you appear?"

...Huh? ...N-No way... How did he know?!

"Wh-What are you talking about?"

"I've heard that true alchemists can create elixirs of immortality and rejuvenation. I always believed they were lies to propel their scams, but if you're a real alchemist, then..."

"I cannot."

Oh, so that's what he meant. Had me scared for a second there.

I displayed my age on my status board.

"I cannot make any elixirs of life or eternal youth. There may be people who can, but it's impossible for me. The most I can do is gather the iron in dirt like this and turn it into ingots."

"I see. I apologize for my assumptions."

That was when Reinhart joined our conversation.

"Now that you believe Ryoma's a real alchemist, let's continue the discussion. As you can see, Ryoma is remarkably able and knowledgeable, and that allows him to make the ingots and waterproof fabric. However, if anyone finds out about his identity as an alchemist, he'd be lumped in with all the other scammers. Furthermore, even if he's recognized for his abilities, his young age will just be looked down upon; there'll be those who try to take advantage of that. That is where I'd like you to step in to buy Ryoma's products at a fair price, Serge. Without publicizing Ryoma as the seller, that is."

"Understood. That would be a piece of cake."

"Ryoma, Serge is a merchant you can trust. If you ever want to sell anything, bring it to this store. It'll be safe to do your shopping here too."

"I understand, thank you very much. I look forward to working with you, Mr. Serge."

"Same here. We will be waiting for Master Ryoma's visits."

"Also, Ryoma? You can use as much dirt from the mines as you wish. You can feed them to your slimes and make ingots for money."

"Are you sure? The profits for you would not be…"

"It's an abandoned mine to begin with, so we never expected any profits anyway. And if you sell your ingots to Serge, we'll profit from the tax. Either way, it won't be a loss to us. The waterproof fabric is predicted to sell well too. You can drop any fabric you make at this store, or any other Morgan Trading Company branch store. Does that sound good, Serge?"

"Yes, that won't be a problem. If Master Ryoma provides his address, I can also arrange for everything to be conducted under utmost secrecy from the closest branch store."

While I was grateful for that, weren't they being a little too nice?

After that, I told a surprised Serge about how I lived in a forest and we decided that I could inform him of my residence after I decided whether I would return there. For the time being, I would use this store while in town. If I was to return to the forest, I could drop the waterproof fabrics off at the branch store in the duke's hometown of Gaunago.

I didn't know how to thank them enough for their kindness... For now, I'd make as much string and ingots as possible while I was in town. If I spent two days crafting with the intent of emptying all my magical energy, I should be able to make a fair amount... Serge had given me a large number of magic replenishing potions as an apology for doubting me anyway.

At any rate, I was glad to have a safe place to sell things. Plus, Serge said I was welcome to drop by for anything. I doubted he would treat me as a fraud.

With everything wrapped up, Serge and his female servant saw us off and we returned to the inn.

⊰ Chapter 2 Episode 8 ⊱
Large-Scale Subjugation Request

The next day.

Eliaria was apparently heading back to the mines to practice over everything she learned yesterday.

As for me, Reinbach asked me to accept the monster subjugation request for the mines that was sent to the Adventurer's Guild today. Eliaria wanted to go with me, but Reinbach and Elise were opposed to that.

What they learned for themselves yesterday was the difference in experience between Eliaria and myself. The large gap in our actual combat abilities, too. On top of it being inefficient in terms of subjugation, there was also the chance the young miss would rely on me too much.

I suppose I did have trouble saying no to her…

And so, I went to the guild, where I was promptly summoned to the guildmaster's office.

"You're here, Ryoma."

"You called for me?"

"It's nothing much. The duke's butler came by just now and put in a monster subjugation request for tomorrow. I'd just like to confirm something about that. Did you go to the mines yesterday?"

"I did."

"Tell me what monsters appeared there. And also the condition of the mines. I've asked the butler for this too, but I'd like to gather as much information as possible."

"I see. I encountered cave mantises, cave bats, and small rats, while Lady Eliaria defeated a slime. There were also metal slimes inside the mines. The mines felt like they had been abandoned for a while; there were weeds everywhere. But the mineshaft I entered felt like it was built properly, and I didn't hear about loose foundations or cave-ins anywhere else, either."

"Then it sounds like G ranks can take on the job without problem. So there were metal slimes too, huh?"

"Yes. I was acting separately at the time, but they captured it for me as a present. I formed a contract with it."

"Oh yeah, I heard you collect all kinds of slimes. Something like over a thousand?"

"That is correct. I currently have 728 sticky slimes, 323 poison slimes, 211 acid slimes, 11 cleaner slimes, 3033 scavenger slimes, 2 healing slimes, 1 metal slime, and 1 regular slime for a total of 4310 slimes."

"That's way too many."

The guildmaster must have expected a smaller number, as he had a rather strained smile on his face.

"The scavenger slimes increased to this number in the incident the other day. Because of that, they split several times in a short time and passed 3000. Slimes can practically survive off nothing but water so they're easy to feed, but if they had been another monster I would have been desperate for food right about now."

"I see... Oh, that's right. There's another request to clean the toilet pits. Please take it if you have the time."

I didn't mind that since I hadn't decided on today's work yet, but wasn't it a bit early?

"It's only been a few days since the last one, though."

"The last request went unattended for so long that we don't know when the next one will be fulfilled! Well, apparently that's what they're thinking, at least. It also came with a threat to send all the complaints our way if we left it sitting for too long. The public office couldn't sway the guys in the slum in the end. Several employees were told 'deal with it,' but they're the same guys that have been slacking until now. Their work just can't live up to yours."

"I see… Got it. How many are there?"

"Thirty cubicles in total. Can you do them all?"

"My slimes have sped up a lot since last time, so if I use the entire day… there should be less to clean than last time too."

"Then I entrust them all to you. The guys from the town are a pain."

"Understood. Oh, what about the procedures for the monster subjugation?"

"It's fine. You can do the procedures for that after you come back today. There's no limit to the number of participants, and I'll put in a word for you."

"All right, then. Ah, is it possible to buy the monsters from the subjugation tomorrow? I could use any kills that don't have material use as food for my slimes."

"If it doesn't seem like it's worth any other value or use, go ahead."

"Thank you very much!"

I rejoiced at the ready agreement I received as I put the guildmaster's office behind me and headed to the same receptionist lady as last time to go through the job procedures. I figured I shouldn't call her the receptionist forever, so I asked for her name and found out it was Maylene.

Furthermore, I also found out that 20 completed jobs was the requirement to advance from G rank to F rank, so the 30 toilet pits I cleaned out last time meant I had fulfilled that. Which meant that from today onwards, I would be treated as an F-rank adventurer.

Incidentally, the advancement requirement to E rank was 30 jobs and one monster subjugation. The ten extra jobs from the previous rank plus today's share would mean I would be an E rank adventurer right after the monster subjugation.

When I asked Maylene whether moving one rank a day was too fast, she answered, "While it certainly seems faster than usual, the monster subjugations up to E rank are all weak monsters that most adults can handle with ease, and the job requests can be completed by anyone. That's why these ranks are more of an observation period for the guild. We look at the jobs you take, your success rate, and the frequency that you accept them to see who's more likely to abandon their job or who only takes a job every now and then but makes sure to do it properly. As long as you take it seriously, the requirements are barely an issue. In that regard, you've never failed a single job and have received nothing but praise so far, so there's no issue here."

So that was that. As I was relieved to hear that I was doing well, I heard a soft mumble just as I was leaving the reception desk.

"Honestly, if only more newcomers were like you… It would be so much more productive if they took on the easy jobs instead of pushing and failing at harder requests…"

Her mutters lingered in my ear.

So it seemed like newbie adventurers normally hated doing odd jobs… Which made sense if they were hot-headed youths. I should take on jobs every now and then to live up to their faith in me.

With that decided, I headed for today's job.

■　■　■

The next day.

The second round of toilet pit cleaning ended without issue, after which I turned in early for the night and woke with time to spare today. The time was 5 in the morning.

After I finished all my morning routines, I still had time to spare. It didn't take much time for a man to prepare in the morning anyway. I spent the time feeding my slimes before leisurely heading out of the inn to the Adventurer's Guild. A huge crowd of adventurers gathered in front of the guild, along with several horse carriages on the road.

"There's a lot more than I expected…"

All the carriages in front of the guild were for transporting the adventurers to the subjugation request. I had heard I could get a free ride if I arrived at the guild before 8, but I hadn't imagined there would be this many people.

If it was too crowded, perhaps I should run there as a morning jog instead? The official meetup time was in front of the mines at 11 or so…

Just as I was pondering what to do, a voice called from far away.

"Hey! Ryoma!"

"Huh? Ah, Jeff!"

The one who had called me was Jeff. Upon further inspection, Leipin and Sher were with him too.

"Good morning, Jeff, Leipin, Sher."

"Yo, morning."

"Good morning, Ryoma."

"Greetings, Ryoma. So you took on this job too."

"Yes, did everyone here take it too?"

"We were nominated by the old man. The request this time should be a safe G-rank one, but we're participating just in case some large monster appears. Miya and Asagi are coming too. Though they've gone ahead."

"There've been large jobs like this before, but the participant numbers this time are especially great…"

"That can't be helped. The monsters in the mines are all easy targets, even for G rankers. The job request came from the lord of the domain himself, so the reward is already decent to begin with, but there's even a bonus reward for bringing the monster corpses back. For low-ranked adventurers, there's no better time to earn money than this."

"But I wonder who would even want to pay for these monster corpses? From what I saw on the confirmed monster list, they're all small fry with no harvestable parts."

"The number of monsters from a subjugation like this is way more than you would need for research, too. It only seems to be beneficial for us, so I must admit I am most curious."

"No, they're not being used for anything impressive. They're just to feed familiars."

"Ryoma, do you know something?"

"Well yes, I'm the one buying the monster corpses."

"Oh my! So the one buying them was you, Ryoma. If you're using them to feed your slimes, everything makes sense. There are… quite a few in your possession, after all…"

"What do you normally do to feed them?"

"They seem like they'd cost a ton to feed. I've heard some familiars cost a fortune to keep."

While we were chatting, a new carriage arrived. Since it was already here, I decided to ride on the carriage with the three of them.

Several hours later.

The carriage arrived safely. The driver told us to check in at the temporary reception set up at the entrance of the mines, so we went to do that before waiting. Once it reached 11, everyone was told to gather in the square.

"The number of participants today is 264! Subjugations take place in parties of six, for safety! No fighting over kills! Anyone who isn't assigned to a party, come this way to check your assigned squads! And finally... earn as much as you can today!"

Everyone cheered at the guildmaster's simple instructions to begin work before gathering into groups and heading into the mines.

...Wait, was that it? I shouldn't be standing around. Which party was I in?

I checked the squad list to see that I was with Jeff, Miya, Welanna, Mizelia, and Cilia. It was comforting to be with people I knew already, but had the guildmaster done that intentionally? At any rate, I had to find them...

I looked around to see five people walking my way with Welanna in the lead.

"Welanna, everyone. I look forward to working with you today."

"Same here, Ryoma."

"Let's do this, nya."

"Let's work hard today."

"I'll be sure to lead you properly, as the more experienced adventurer."

"That's impossible for you, Mizelia. We saw each other just earlier, but hey again."

"Wha— Hey, Jeff! Isn't that a bit rude?!"

"You might have the skills, but you're too hasty."

"What was that?!"

"What are you two on about... Ryoma, ignore those two. Now, time for combat checks. Ryoma, what's your weapon? Cave bats and small rats should be easy, but have you fought cave mantises before?"

"I've fought them before. I normally use a bow and arrow, but I can use daggers and martial arts too. The rest of the time I use magic."

"Then Ryoma, please focus on using your magic to attack the airborne enemies. Since no one else in our party can use attack magic."

"It's not that we can't use it at all, nya! It's just that beastkin have less magical energy, so you can't really rely on our magic, nya. Though Cilia has more magical energy than the average beastkin..."

"Unfortunately, I can only use healing magic."

"Mizelia and I are terrible at magic in general. We've given up on everything but the neutral spells for enhancement and hardening!"

"Don't lump me together with you, I *excel* in enhancement and hardening!"

"That's just a different way of saying the same thing, nya... So what element do you use, Ryoma?"

"All of them, but I mostly use earth."

"All elements! That's rare, nya."

"There's more variation in your fighting that way. By earth, you mean Earth Needle?"

"Earth Needle and Rock Bullet. Out of the other elements, the only things I can really use inside a mine would be Ice Arrow and Stun Arrow, I guess."

"That's more than enough. All right, let's go!"

Thus the subjugation began.

∼ Chapter 2 Episode 9 ∼
An Average Adventurer

"There's no challenge…"

We stepped into a new mineshaft all pumped up, but the monsters that appeared were all so weak, we proceeded forward smoothly. This was already the third mineshaft.

"What challenge is there to seek from small rats and slimes?"

"If a challenging enemy to Jeff appeared it'd just be trouble, nya. We'd be fine, but the other G and F rankers would be in danger."

"Our main job is to be prepared in case the worst happens in the mines."

"It's just that only standing around sets a bad example to the lower ranks."

Based on their words and fighting until now — especially the fighting — these people were far more skilled than the bandits I had encountered in this world until now. Were they actually really high-ranked people? Why was I mixed into a group with them?

"Hmm? Something the matter, Ryoma?"

"No, it's just that everyone here seems to be high-ranked, so I was wondering why an F-rank like me was grouped with you. Was the guildmaster being considerate? It's easier around familiar faces, after all."

"That's not it. The old man likes to meddle, but he prioritizes ability when it comes to jobs."

"It's probably because the five of us would struggle against a monster only weak to magic, so he valued your stamina and strength."

"Ryoma. We're actually moving at a fairly fast pace right now, one that an F-rank adventurer would normally be unable to keep up with."

"At first, I was planning on dropping our pace once Ryoma showed signs of fatigue. But he's been keeping up without issue the whole time."

Really? I hadn't noticed at all.

"Ryoma, you're not actually F-rank in ability, are you? There's no way."

"What's the biggest monster you defeated until now?"

"The biggest one wasn't a monster, but a black bear that inhabits the Forest of Gana."

The five of them looked as though their expectations were confirmed.

"There's no way a normal F ranker could defeat a black bear, nya. Even D rankers have to team up to hunt one safely."

"If you hunted a black bear alone, that would put you at the combat ability of a C-rank adventurer. You've shown the guildmaster your skill before, right?"

Come to think of it, yes.

"When I was registering, the guildmaster supervised my entry test."

"That would be it."

"No mistake there. He must have had his eye on you since then."

"That's why he put you in this squad. Makes sense."

"You have the ability, so don't let ranks bother you, nya. You'll climb up to the same rank as us in no time."

"Speaking of which, what rank is everyone? I haven't heard yet."

"Didn't we mention it?"

"We're all B rank."

"A rank just barely worthy of calling ourselves top-class adventurers."

"For the record, Sher who you met earlier is D rank, and Gordon is B rank. Asagi and Leipin are both A rank."

We were walking and talking when Welanna came to a sudden stop, focusing her attention in front of her. She seemed to be scenting something.

"What's wrong?"

"From the smell of things, there's a colony of cave bats up ahead. There's so many of them. It's not dangerous, but some will definitely get away before we can defeat them all."

"How bothersome, nya…"

"Are there any people on the other side?"

"There's no smell like that. Can you use some kind of wide-range attack magic?"

"It's not a killing one, but I have something that will work perfectly."

I explained the Sound Bomb I tested yesterday.

"Huh, you can do something like that?"

"I've never heard of that magic before."

Well, I would hope not, since I made it with knowledge from Earth.

"That magic can only knock them out or render them immobile, right? Will we be able to finish off all the cave bats before they revive?"

"It'd be a lot easier after knocking them out, but I'm not sure if we'll make it in time."

91

"Then how about we ask the people behind us?"

The five of them agreed to my suggestion.

"Wait, you noticed too?"

"I lived in the forest for three years, after all. I'm sensitive to presences."

"I see. In that case, let's wait here for a bit."

So... there was actually a group of six people that had been following us from a distance all this time. They didn't seem particularly aggressive so we had ignored them until now, but according to the others they were probably poor G- to E-rank adventurers. They were probably picking up the monsters we threw aside for money.

According to Welanna, the rewards for G- to E-rank jobs were low, so it was common for newbie adventurers to struggle financially with the costs of living and equipment.

"Unless they have some other kind of income, their living costs only settle once they start D-rank jobs."

"Until then, they have lots of expenses, nya. Every injury and unforeseen circumstance costs."

"There are many people that save up in advance, but how long they take to rank up depends on their work. Oftentimes someone will mess up doing an unfamiliar task, and their money runs out before advancement."

"In exchange, once you can complete D-rank requests steadily, you should be able to receive enough money to compensate for those expenses, while C rank would bring about a comfortable lifestyle. That was how Miya bought her home, too. I think she was a little hasty with that home, but there aren't many jobs for people of our age that allow us to buy our own homes. It's a clear example of how some adventurer jobs are high risk, high return."

Like Cilia had said, Miya still looked to be in her early twenties. I don't know how many years it's been since she bought her house, but she was about the age of a university student in Japan. To buy her own house with money she earned working at that age... It was actually quite amazing. Hell, I myself only lived in a run-down apartment up until my death... Though I couldn't complain about it.

"At B rank and above, all the jobs become dangerous and fewer in number, but the rewards rocket up. As long as you don't spend recklessly or slack off, you won't have an issue with money. But up until E rank, the low risk makes for the worst financial struggle. That's why the people behind us now are probably under D rank."

For this subjugation request, the monsters belonged to whomever finished them off. But if adventurers couldn't hold any more, they would discard them starting from the most worthless ones. Discarded monsters were seen as abandoned items, so other adventurers would gather them for money.

But while this behavior wasn't forbidden, it wasn't favorable either. It could also cause issues later, so it was a bit of a gray zone for those who did it without permission.

We rested where we were for a while, until the party in question noticed us resting and stopped. That was when Welanna called out to them loudly.

"You lot over there! We know you've been following us this whole time! Show your faces!"

The six of them panicked, but eventually appeared.

Four humans and two beastkin, huh... This might be rude to say, but they overall looked quite shabby. They must be adventurers struggling with living costs... But they were pretty young. They didn't seem much older than me, perhaps?

"What are you lot shadowing us for, hmm?"

"We were… picking up discarded monsters…"

"…First off, we're not trying to pick a fight with you."

The six faces brightened a little, relieved at those words.

"But I'd like to hear why you chose to do such a thing, yeah?"

"Y-Yes ma'am! The truth is, we're all G and F ranks… and don't have much money…"

"I was doing okay in the start, but after buying weapons and armor, I ran out of money…"

"I messed up a subjugation job and lost all my money paying the contract penalty…"

"We were struggling to feed ourselves, making do by living frugally. Then, when this job came up, we jumped at the chance. We figured we could earn enough to cover our living expenses for a while. The monsters are weak, so it's safe, and we get paid for participating and bringing back monster bodies. We just knew we had to make as much as we could!"

"That was when we saw you guys come this way, and…"

The reasons they gave were exactly as had been explained to me just now. It must be really common, huh… I listened quietly as Jeff pressed the human girl to continue.

"And what?"

"And…"

"We saw that kid following you. We figured if you were willing to take a kid like that into the mines with you, then you wouldn't mind if we took the monsters you discarded. We thought people that could put up with a kid that was a clear hindrance would let us off lightly."

The other five people looked rather uncomfortable at the boy's words. Of course they would. I was still a member of this party, and it would normally be rude to call someone outright useless.

However, the other five must have also felt the same or agreed to it, as not a single person bothered to stop or argue against him.

"Do you lot realize the position you're in—"

Welanna started to scold them for looking down on me when I stopped her. This stuff didn't bother me, and there was nothing to be done about it.

"It's fine, Welanna."

"Ryoma, it's better to speak your mind in times like this."

"Thoughts can't always be changed just by talking. I can't help my weak appearance."

"Fine... But! You lot! If that was the case, why didn't you say anything? Grabbing them without a word makes you no different to thieves!"

""We're very sorry!!""

After the six of them apologized, they tried to offer the monsters they had taken back to us, but Cilia and Mizelia put a stop to that.

"Hold it! We took issue with you guys for collecting the corpses without telling us, not for actually collecting the corpses."

"If you're strapped for cash, you can take it. We don't need it anyway. But if you're going to do this, make sure you get permission next time."

"If you're too ashamed to ask for permission, don't do it from the beginning. Train yourselves until you don't have to!"

The six of them brightened at those words. They thanked everyone other than me. Welanna looked a little unhappy at that, but Miya began to ask the six of them for help as planned.

"There's actually another reason why we called out to you, nya. There's a colony of cave bats up ahead, but there's too many for us to take out quickly. So, could you help us, nya? You can keep the corpses, nya!"

Naturally, they were on board with that. While I was using Probe to confirm no one else was around, Miya gave a simple explanation of the plan to them.

"First, Ryoma will fire a magic into the back of the cave. Then we charge in, nya."

"Wouldn't that kid's magic just make the enemy more alert?"

The other party expressed their apprehension, but backed down when Welanna yelled at them to go home if they had complaints. But they still whispered to each other a small distance away. About their doubts towards me, and how they should do it for the money anyway, I suppose.

I paid them no mind as I finished my checks and set up the soundproof barrier.

"I'm ready."

"All right. Do it, Ryoma. You lot, get ready to move!"

"Here I go! *Sound Bomb!*"

I activated my magic and set off the sound explosion in the mineshaft. But the noise didn't reach us thanks to the soundproof barrier. The low-rank party took that to mean it failed.

"Nothing happened?"

"It probably failed."

"It was a success, you just can't see it because it's wind magic."

After saying that, Welanna and everyone made their way into the cave, followed by the six skeptical adventurers.

Once they reached the depths, they stared at the floor in a daze. An immense number of cave bats were piled on the floor.

"They're only knocked out, so please split up and finish them off quickly," I said as I got straight to work. After we finished off all the cave bats, we realized that we were at the end of the mineshaft and exited, leaving the other party behind us. They could at least clean up the rest, since that would benefit them more.

But that was when Welanna asked me, "Ryoma, was it really okay not to say anything to them?"

"I believe I showed enough with that single spell. If they can't accept the truth with that, speaking would have been a waste of time."

"That may be true…"

In the first place, things like this could only be resolved when dealing with people who could accept facts; those who only wanted to complain wouldn't listen anyway. Even if they were the latter type, I could just avoid associating with them in the future. Changing someone was a feat that took time and effort — if it worked at all. Those that didn't change would never do so, no matter how much time passed. You simply had to be prepared to cut those people out… in my opinion.

"They didn't seem to have any money, so let's just say it was the desperate struggles of some brazen young boys and girls to live and call it a day."

"Brazen young… You talk like you're so much older than them, Ryoma. You know the oldest of them is fifteen, right?"

"Are you really 11, Ryoma?"

"If that's what Ryoma decided then fine, nya."

Anyway, even if my body was a child my heart was still a 42-year-old old man… I didn't feel like scolding some kids over such trivial matters, and the others had already lectured them enough. I also showed them my magic skills already. All that was left was for them to reflect for themselves.

"But I am a little curious. Do I really look that weak?"

I did survive three years in the forest relying mostly on my physical strength, and fought with bandits too. …It actually bothered me quite a bit, now that I think about it.

"You don't really look strong, yeah."

In my previous life, the young ones at the company would backbite me by saying my presence had them feeling like they were on the hot seat. Was it really my appearance after all?

"Let's see… I already know you're strong after seeing you fight today, but seeing you like this out of combat doesn't really give a 'strong' impression…"

"It might be rude to put it like this, but it's like you're missing that certain aura… Of course, I already knew about your stamina and hunting skills, so I wasn't worried about you being a hindrance. But I had no clue about your skills…"

"After reaching a certain level of strength, you're supposed to be able to tell how strong another person is to a degree, nya…"

"Honestly, your fighting was more adept than I expected, too. I was surprised."

"Aura is a perception thing so some people may have duller or sharper senses for it, but us beastkin should be on the sharp end. And yet, Ryoma's aura is all over the place… Are you hiding your ability?"

"No, not intentionally."

I didn't have to keep up appearances as much as my last life, so I didn't particularly bother with that. At most, I avoided making any actions that could be seen as threatening, but that was more within the realms of common sense than concealment.

"Then it might just be your individuality. What they call human nature."

"You really think so? Whenever I saw bandits in the forest, they always looked down on me. Though I always turned the tables on them."

"I get how you feel. Also, those bandits were pretty unlucky."

"That must have felt like hunting slimes, nya…"

"The ones that actually appeared were tougher than black bears, though."

"Cilia's right… Does that make Ryoma a natural trap?"

Before I knew it, I was being treated as bandit bait.

Apparently it had reached lunchtime while we were talking, so we decided to return to the square.

～ Chapter 2 Episode 10 ～
Monster Subjugation Break Time

"Thank you for the meal."

During lunch break. In the corner of the square where the adventurers gathered to eat the distributed lunches, I finished eating. But from what I could see around me, the others were still eating.

All the time spent eating alone had trained me to eat fast without realizing it. It was a habit from my previous life, but... What should I do now? Jeff and Welanna had gone to eat with the other adventurers to gather information...

Finding myself idle, I thought about what to do for a moment before deciding to tend to my slimes.

"Excuse me."

I called out to an employee at the temporary reception where they were collecting information and organizing non-subjugation work.

"Oh hello, Ryoma."

"Good day, Miss Maylene. Do you have a moment?"

"Sure, what's up?"

"Just letting you know I'm going to step away for a bit to feed my slimes. Can I collect the harvested monsters yet?"

"They've been gathered on the other side. You're free to take them. You've paid in advance already, so if the guild employees ask anything just show them your guild card. I have received your notice of individual action. Take care. Make sure you're back before the end of lunch, okay?"

"There's a roll call by squad, right?"

"Yup. If you end up running late, come to the temporary reception first. This is a countermeasure against pay thieves that leave halfway, so if you skip this step you'll be marked for abandonment and lose your reward."

"I understand. Thank you very much."

After Maylene's warning, I left the reception and went to pick up four baskets of monster bodies before leaving the square.

"Around here should do... *Dimension Home*."

I walked for a while and reached the top of a steep hill with a clear overlook and no signs of other people. I'd notice any approaching monsters or people easily from here.

After watching over the slimes that crawled out of the wide, white hole in space, I began feeding them the monster corpses.

First, I let the cleaner slimes eat the filth, then split the remainder into four. Next to the four piles, I prepared four large containers filled with water. Once I gave the signal, the poison, sticky, acid and scavenger slimes — in their big or huge forms — climbed onto the pile of food and devoured it.

I kept an eye on their energetic feasting while I prepared the metal slime's meal as well. As I was doing that, the metal slime had used its hard body to dig a hole in the ground and eat the dirt.

So, it could gain iron content from eating dirt... though it wasn't digging well.

It looked more like it was throwing a tantrum at going unfed rather than digging. I sped up my work and placed a container of iron-content dirt on the floor, at which point it gave up digging and approached at super-slow speed. I could tell it was trying to hurry through the contract, but it was truly slow. Maybe its metal body was slow?

I sat beside the metal slime as it ate and watched over it, leisurely letting the time pass. For the record, healing slimes gained their energy through photosynthesis, so they had been sunbathing behind me the entire time.

After the slimes' meal.

There was something I was curious about, so I sent all except one of the poison, sticky, and acid slimes back into the Dimension Home.

"Thanks."

I had the three slimes spit out the liquid in their bodies onto a plate, filling each plate with poison, sticky solution, and acid.

The metal slime had a hard body, and it even had Harden as a skill. I could tell it was strong against physical attacks, but what about poison? I didn't know. And so I was experimenting.

That being said, I was just going to let the slime approach the plates and watch its reaction... First was the poison plate.

"...Seems fine, huh?"

The metal slime didn't even twitch. A sticky slime would have backed away... but it didn't move at all. It seemed as unaffected as a poison slime itself. Next was the sticky solution.

"...This one's fine too."

The metal slime continued showing no reaction until the next acid plate. As it approached, its body flattened as though it was melting before it wriggled and backed away slowly.

"So you're bad with acid... Reminds me of my science projects..."

There was an experiment to put hydrochloric acid on metal leaves or something... sure brings back memories.

I didn't want to scare it too much, so the experiment ended there. I moved the plates away and disposed of them, after which the metal slime returned to its original shape. But because it had tried to flee in a panic, its body was covered in dust.

…I should wipe it away.

I used a handkerchief to wipe it when I realized it was slowly following my hand movements to change shape. It was an impossible texture to feel on normal metal, which made it all the more fascinating. Before I knew it, I was molding the metal slime into a sphere like a child playing with mud balls.

"All right! Oops, should I be heading back now…?"

I checked the clock I previously received. It was about time to head off if I wanted to go back without rushing.

Time to return the slimes to the Dimension Home… Just as I tried to do that, I placed the metal slime on the ground.

The normally distorted metal lump was currently a very round sphere. And this was the top of a hill.

"Dimension Ho—?!"

A high pitched noise attracted my attention, and I looked over to see a ball rolling from the hill at a great speed. With a gasp, I looked to my feet to see the metal slime missing.

"Wai—"

I reflexively started to give chase when I remembered the three slimes I had left out.

If an adventurer came across them…

I hurriedly picked them up before giving chase to the metal slime that had rolled fairly far away in the span of a few seconds.

Even a human could die if they fell and hit themselves in the wrong place. And slimes were creatures that could die even without that. Which is what I believed to be the reason for their soft bodies.

Though this one had a sturdier body through evolution, I was still worried.

Before long, the metal slime came to a stop at the overgrown weeds at the foot of the hill. But the slime itself wasn't moving.

"Are you okay?"

I ran over to check. The metal slime's surface was gradually rippling. It seemed like the shock of the new experience had caused it to harden.

That scared me... Next time I should investigate how much of an impact metal can take. If I avoided the core and just tested on the metal part... No, I should increase their numbers first just to be safe.

With that decided, I picked the metal slime up.

"...! ....?"

"...!!"

"Hmm?"

A voice? I could only just hear it if I listened carefully, but it wasn't my imagination. It was a person's voice — a number of people's voices. The direction... was towards the square. It must have been some adventurers on the job.

But it sounded like the voices were fighting? I couldn't make out the details, but it sounded vaguely threatening.

"I'm curious... let's take a look."

Even if I were to report trouble to the guildmaster or reception, it wouldn't help much if I didn't know what it was about.

Having decided to take a detour, I placed the sticky slime on my head and the poison and acid slime on each shoulder as I began walking silently.

I found it.

I headed in the direction of the quarreling voices until I had pretty much reached the foot of the mines. The trees there blocked the light from shining through, creating a dim corner where armed adventurers gathered around, adjacent to a pile of red dirt discarded from the cliff. There were over ten adventurers present. I couldn't see through the shadow of the spoil tip, but they were surrounding something there.

"You brats better knock it off already!"

"Nothing more than pathetic thieves, stealing other people's kills!"

The men in the outer circle jeered. Was their rough tone due to their anger, or were they just a vulgar lot to begin with? Either way, the situation seemed quite tense.

Was it a fight?

"We're not thieves! We were allowed to take them!"

Huh? That voice sounded kind of familiar...

Brats, thieves stealing kills, a familiar voice... A vague memory resurfaced from those factors.

Could it be...?

Taking care of the wind direction as though I was out hunting, I moved through the trees and grass to circle around the back of the men. I drew closer until the fifty meter mark, at which point it was unmistakable.

Three girls were huddled together in the gap between two spoil tips, sandwiched with the cliff behind them and the men before them. The three boys in their group stood in front of them, acting as a wall. They were all clearly frightened as they tried to cover each other, standing up to the men closing in on them.

Their identities were as I expected — the group of young adventurers following us in the mineshaft earlier.

...Huh? Who was at fault here, though?

"Don't get cocky, you filthy slum brats!"

Just how did things turn out like this... While the air was tense, they fortunately hadn't turned to physical violence yet. They weren't bandits that would suddenly turn to weapons, so I could observe a little longer.

Having over ten grown men surround and yell at children wasn't a nice sight, but I was curious to what the six kids had done.

They were... or at least had been, picking up kills without permission. If they had been doing that in front of these men, then the men might not be at fault. Even if the act was borderline not counted as thievery, an apology would still be reasonable to demand.

Although I did find this interrogation by outnumbering method rather questionable.

We — or rather, everyone apart from me — had also called them out before, but that was just so Jeff could give them a warning for their own good. We hadn't blocked their escape route and yelled. There was a big difference in contempt and the freedom of mind and body going on here.

In reality, the kids had conversed with us before, but they were practically silent now. The guys yelling at them already seemed like they were a hair's breadth away from throwing fists.

It would be best to call someone over who could calm this scene down, but I couldn't reach the square in a single Warp... I couldn't teleport others like Sebas and Leipin yet either. Risking an accident was out of the question. If I relied on anyone else, I'd have to go through the trouble of explaining this location.

Out of that group, there only seemed to be people prepared to fight kids and people prepared to watch on with pitying eyes... I didn't have much time.

It may seem like I'm just spectating too, but I had the confidence I could stop things if I needed to by remaining here.

What to do...

When I thought about it that way, I felt better staying here. But that meant I couldn't call for others.

If I called over someone high-ranking, I could leave it to them. However, there was no guarantee the boys and girls would be safe.

It's easy to be alone until things like this happen...

When I lived alone in the forest, no one ever rushed me. But now, I was feeling the inconvenience of lacking help.

Hmm... There were a total of twelve men surrounding them. They all seemed like young men in their twenties. But there was one bearded man that looked like he was in his thirties.

He was the only one that looked formidable, the rest didn't look that strong. Not even the bearded man had noticed I was hiding, so the bandits I'd faced until now seemed much worse than them. They weren't too dangerous.

But they were unmistakably stronger than the other six. If they fought in this situation, the six kids would be clearly outnumbered and outmatched. There was no chance for self-defense here.

"Oi! Why don't ya say something?!"

...Well, if they had been stealing, then 10 to 20 blows should do the trick. That was the natural punishment to receive back when I was young. Though modern day Japan would greatly oppose it, this was another world. It was a perfectly reasonable way of disciplining children.

Thievery would normally be handed to the Adventurer's Guild or public safety agency as a crime to be judged by the law, so a couple of blows was a kind compromise in comparison.

Even if it was over behavior that didn't quite count as a crime, Jeff and the others had already warned them before lunch. If they continued in spite of that, then they should solve this themselves. It would be pointless for me to step forward when I had only met them once.

Though I wouldn't allow them to go too far. And blows would only be acceptable if they had actually committed the crime; if they hadn't done anything then there was no need to hit them.

Was it the children's fault after all? But what if it wasn't... I tried to determine that from the conversation, but they were repeating the same words over and over like a broken record.

...It would be faster to ask them myself. Okay, let's do that.

I set only the unrefined metal slime down at my feet before standing.

"Excuse me!"

"?!"

"Who's there?!"

"Over there!"

"A slime?! A talking slime?!"

"Look again, dumbass! There's a head below it!"

"Why does this brat have three slimes on him?"

"How long has he been here for?!"

"Sorry to interrupt you."

I parted my way through the bushes and stepped forward, meeting the dubious looks of the men with no hesitation. At the same time, the boys and girls also spotted me. One of the girls unthinkingly opened her mouth.

"Ah, you're…"

When that mutter reached the ears of the men surrounding them, their expressions twisted with creepy smiles.

"Oh, you're one of their friends?"

"No, I'm just passing by," I replied bluntly, making the men look skeptical.

"From what I can see, everyone here is participating in the monster subjugation job, is that correct? It's almost time to gather in the square again, but I was walking past when I heard you all arguing."

"Really? It seemed like these guys know you."

"You're not another thief, are ya?"

"You're packin' some awful nice armor for a brat."

The men started to evaluate me. Their eyes were clearly fixed on my equipment.

"I met the six of them in a mineshaft before lunch. Were they stealing again?"

"That's right. That they were."

"We were not! They're lying!"

"His squad let us take the monsters!"

"We didn't steal any of your kills!"

"Oh, shut up!"

"What proof do you have?! None, right?!"

"They're telling the truth. My party agreed to give them the kills before lunch. If you cannot believe me, then we can go and meet the other members of my team. Everyone else in the party are accomplished adventurers, so I think you'll find them trustworthy. As I mentioned just now, it's almost time to gather again, so it would be perfect timing."

I stated facts to the two yelling sides and made a suggestion, but the men's side changed attitudes when they heard it.

"Th-That would be causing trouble to your party…"

"This is our problem to deal with."

"You're not trying to buy time to wipe the evidence, are ya?!"

"It may just be your plot to cling to someone with a sob story to sway them! As if we'd believe you!"

"We just want to resolve things peacefully too."

"If we made a huge deal of it, they'd have trouble finding jobs in the future too, y'know?"

I understood their words, but the atmosphere and their attitudes reminded me of younger guys who would try and hide their own mistakes. They just didn't want other people to butt in.

As the men objected to taking the matter elsewhere to be resolved, the impartiality within me started to lean towards the six kids instead. That was when one man who had been observing until now spoke up.

"I agree with the kid, there's no point in continuing this conversation here."

"Sacchi?!"

The bearded man named Sacchi spoke up. It seemed like he was the leader after all, as the others fell silent. Well, he did seem the strongest.

"You sure have guts for a kid. But how did you get so close without us noticing? I had my guard up for monsters and all."

"I used to support myself through hunting, so I'm good at hiding."

"I see… You lot, there's no point in arguing any further. Like that brat said, it's almost time to gather. So let's put an end to this."

Similar words to my own left Sacchi's mouth. His attitude was so dauntless, it was hard to imagine him as the leader of that rowdy group of adventurers. The men that had been yelling earlier showed no signs of defying him.

Then, the men that had been blocking the way before the six kids snorted as they each...

Drew their weapons.

～ Chapter 2 Episode 11 ～
Unruly Adventurers

"Earth Fence."

"Nwah?!"

"Yowch!"

Stone posts the height of two adults shot out of the ground, separating the six kids from the men that had shown their true colors.

One man had been caught by a post and was lifted alongside them, but he fell the moment he flailed about. The sudden appearance of the fence had them backing away warily. I deliberately stepped into the space that opened up. It saved me the trouble of having the kids taken as hostages.

"Oww, what happened…?"

"It's magic!"

"What is this magic? Is it your doing?!"

"You drew your weapons, so I acted reflexively. This spell is called Earth Fence. It repeatedly uses a magic called Earth Needle to create the individual posts of a fence. As a result, the top of the fence is a little sharp… If that person had been one step closer it would have made a gory sight. Thank goodness it didn't come to that."

I explained the magic as a distraction to the situation, making several people including the man that was lifted up stiffen in expression at the image.

That aside, even though the leader had said the same things as me about wasting time, gathering at the square, and ending this…

They had taken his words in a completely different way. Language sure was difficult!

...Well, jokes aside, it seemed like these people were fairly used to this kind of business. At first, the men had drawn their weapons to point to me, but two of them had pointed them at the six kids. They were probably going to use them as hostages.

Even before Sacchi gave the command, no one had discussed anything. Which meant they had either planned this in advance, or were so used to this situation they didn't need to discuss it at all.

Though they were adventurers with rough jobs, their speech was bandit-like, and their movements clearly weren't adapted for only monsters. It was looking clear to me that these men were at fault here, but they could have other crimes too.

"Don't give me those pathetic excuses, you morons."

"Boss..."

"A brat's magic won't amount to much. Stop him from using it and he's finished. Are you guys so weak you'd turn tail and run from a single brat? I ain't got no use for weaklings like that."

"H-Hey... Hey!"

Hm?

As Sacchi was reprimanding his underlings, the shortest human boy from the group of six whispered at me. He was grabbing the posts of the fence and leaning his body out like a jail cell, but I clearly remembered him as the boy that called me a hindrance.

"Run away! These guys are serious. Even if you're good at magic, you can't go up against their numbers."

It seemed like he had accepted my magic skills, but he still considered me weaker than this lot.

"In that case, you should prepare to run too," I said using the wind magic Whisper, adding that I'd remove the fence when I had the chance.

However, it wasn't easy to discuss things before the enemy's eyes.

Perhaps they had heard the whispering words I sent to the kids, or maybe they had noticed the kids' change in attitude, but Sacchi gave another order.

"Oi, you lot watching over there! You help too. The brat said he's good at running and hiding."

"Hehehe. Thanks, Boss."

"Too bad for you, huh? If only you hadn't come this way."

"No point in saying this now, but we woulda let you off easy if you had just handed over the money quietly, y'know?"

"Was it a lie that they stole your kills?"

"No, we consider them stolen. Those brats are from the slums. People who take from others when they're strapped for cash."

"If you're willing to pay in their place, we'll let ya go. You seem much richer than those brats, after all."

"With armor like that, you must be. We take payment plans too, y'know? If you can't pay up now, how about we go to your parents directly?"

At Sacchi's words, the people who had been observing with the weapons sheathed hesitantly drew them, making the men even more arrogant.

…What a pain in the ass.

There had been bandits that looked down on me for being a child, but even they hadn't pissed me off as much as the men before me. This may actually be the most irritated I've been since coming to this world. I didn't know the reason why I was affected so much… Was he just asking for it?

My parents were long dead in my past life, and I didn't have any in this one. If anything, I had the stand-in parents Gain and the other gods prepared. They were dead too, so my only options were the dead, or the gods. Out of these two options, neither could be consulted directly.

I was indebted to the duke's family, but there was no way I was letting them pay people like this. Before that, they wouldn't even be able to meet them. I wouldn't let them.

I glared at the men who were overconfident in their numbers. But just then...

"W-Wait!"

One of the formerly observing adventurers said. Everyone turned their cold gazes at the young man that had interrupted, but he was panicking with no care for them.

I... haven't done anything yet, though...?

"That kid — isn't he the one from the rumors lately?! You shouldn't touch him!"

"...Oh, yeah. There was talk about a kid with slimes showing up at the guild."

"Wasn't it about a brat loitering around the guild and town in weird clothes?"

"What about it?"

"Are you just chickening out from fighting?"

The men that had drawn their weapons early sneered at the young man.

"Someone said they saw the kid in the weird clothes enter the high-class inn that the duke was staying at! He might be involved with them, you know?!"

"A brat like this?"

"No way someone like that would be here."

"Hey... Wasn't the client for today's request... the duke...?"

"N-No way!"

"But I did hear that the duke was staying in Gimul Town... The public office got hit with a heavy penalty recently too..."

His panic suddenly made sense. The reason why he hadn't followed his friends' example was because he feared the wrath of the duke. Though it was a little too late for that...

However, his suspicion and confusion spread, giving us the perfect chance.

There were exactly six enemies to the left and the right, and the square was to the left. The six kids... were ready. Time to go!

"*Create Block.*"

"Oi!"

I changed the ground beneath the fence into a lump of stone and enhanced myself and the fence. Ignoring Sacchi's voice, I pulled out a fence post and swung it to the left.

"Stop!"

"Gah!"

The post turned into a large blunt weapon, sending three men flying.

"Run now! That way!"

"Right!"

"Don't let the brats get away."

"Hold up! Grr!"

This time, angry yelling faces closed in from the right, so I swung the post that way.

"Hah?!"

"Wai—?!"

Five of the men after me were squished under the stone lump like flies. The only one that got away was Sacchi, who glared this way menacingly as he held his axe at the ready as I flung the slimes on my shoulders to the left.

"!"

To prevent the two men who escaped from the blow earlier from attacking the kids, I had thrown two slimes at the sides of their faces. They reflexively tried to defend themselves by swinging their swords, but it was ineffective without reaching the core.

A sticky splashing sound echoed rather loudly as the two slimes clung to the swords. The next moment, screams roared throughout the vicinity.

"Geh! Urgh! My body… my feet…"

"Gaaah! My arms are…! They're…?!"

The slimes I had thrown were poison and acid. They had released their poison and acid respectively to gnaw away at them.

"You little…!"

A single-edged axe came swinging for my neck. But I avoided it by distancing myself.

"You've done it now, brat…"

What happened to his confidence earlier?

Veins were popping in Sacchi's red face as he swung his axe.

"How long are you idiots gonna sleep for?! Get up and catch 'em already!"

The men pinned under the fence post crawled out. Those that had been mowed down with the first blow held their bodies as they stood up. The exception was the one man hit by poison.

"Don't stop! Keep running!"

It would help me too if they ran away faster. I yelled at the six kids that were about to stop, and they gave me one more look before scampering away.

"Damn it! You'd best catch 'em or die trying! Whether this brat is connected to the duke or not, you know what'll happen if they tell the guild! Newbies abandon jobs all the time, catch 'em and teach 'em a lesson!"

"B-But Boss... This is bad!"

Because I had prioritized opening a path, the men who were standing weren't seriously injured. But they were getting cold feet. It seemed like they lost all their attitude along with their advantage.

"I'll do it. It doesn't matter if the duke's backing him. I'll educate him so he won't go crying to them. That's what I made you practice all that healing magic for, no?"

"But..."

"Shaddap! There's no other choice! Follow my lead!"

Sacchi yelled, then swung his axe with a roar. He closed the distance between us like a beast. His aim was my collar, huh? He didn't seem to have any killing intent, as he was swinging with the blunt end of his axe. But even without the blade pointed this way, it was a blunt metal weapon. There was enough force behind it to break a human body.

I stepped forward and used my left arm to knock Sacchi's axe-wielding right arm off course.

"?!"

His right elbow had been straightened as he was swinging down, so I wound my right arm around it and kicked the back of his right knee. That was enough to knock him off balance, and when he fell to his knees I fortified my arm, allowing me to witness his shell-shocked expression as he went down. I added strength into my fortified arm until I heard a dull sound from his shoulder.

"Gaah?! Oww!"

When I released Sacchi's arm, it dangled down loosely. He dropped the axe he was holding, no longer able to pick it up.

Sweating through the pain, he attempted a backhand blow with his left hand. But it was pathetically weak. I grabbed his hand and stepped on his kneeling right leg, putting strength into it. After a sensation like stepping on a twig, I also broke Sacchi's left arm with a hand chop.

"...!! Guuhh..."

"...Huh?"

"Boss..."

"Was wiped out in an instant...?"

Sacchi collapsed with a groan, bending over the ground. Two broken bones and one dislocation must have hurt, but that one must have been his pride. I doubt he expected this situation. The other adventurers behind him had all frozen with stiff looks.

"Who would like to go next?"

I said with a beaming smile.

"U-Uh... We'll pass..."

"!"

"Ah?!"

"Hey! Don't flee without us!"

"*Teleport.*"

I appeared before the man who tried to run.

"Where do you think you're going?"

"Eek?!"

"Space magic?!"

"Just what is this guy?!"

"Forgive us! We couldn't defy Sacchi's orders!"

"Please save those words for the guildmaster. For now... I don't want you chasing after the kids that got away, so you're staying here with me for a bit longer."

After that, I listened to the wails of the disorderly gang as I spent a surprisingly long amount of time restraining them with my slimes' power, just in case.

I was definitely late for the gathering time.

⌁ Chapter 2 Episode 12 ⌁
Monster Subjugation at the Mines, End of Day 1

"That should do it."

After I set enough countermeasures against the unruly adventurers' escape, I got ready to go call for help when two sets of footsteps approached. I was a little wary of more enemies, but I soon relaxed.

"It seems thou hast has already settled things?"

"Asagi! Leipin! What are you two doing here?"

"A panicked youngling came crying for help, stating they had been cornered by a group of ill-natured adventurers and left someone behind to hold them off."

Those kids must have called for help, huh?

"He mentioned slimes, so I got to thinking… So it was you after all, Ryoma. I'm glad you're safe. What happened over there?"

"It doesn't seem like the other party is dead… Though there is no movement."

The two said, looking at the adventurers I restrained.

In order to prevent the unruly adventurers from fleeing when I left, and to also act as their treatment, their limbs had been fitted with a plaster of sticky slime hardening solution over splints and a mouth gag made of stone with breathing holes had been inserted into their mouths, before I paralyzed them with poison to restrict movement.

Finally, to prevent them from being attacked by monsters, I made my slimes surround them as guards... But there may have been a few too many.

"They look like they've been buried alive..."

"Hmm... I shall watch over here. Ryoma, thou should move the slimes and return to the reception. Jeff and the others await you."

"Oh! In that case, I should hurry."

"I shall go make a report too. I'll bring you with me with my magic."

I took Leipin up on his word.

Despite being slightly surprised by them, I quickly moved all my slimes back into the Dimension Home.

I was truly late right now.

Thus, after returning to the reception and explaining everything to the receptionist, I was ordered to return to work.

I passed the guildmaster on my way out and was told I'd be informed of my penalty later. And so, what I had to do now was...

"I'm sorry for being late."

I apologized to the five people in my party for my tardiness.

They had heard the situation already, so no one was really angry and just teased me a little.

Then, after work.

As adventurers piled into the return carriages one after another, I was summoned by the guildmaster.

"You're here... Well, have a seat."

The guildmaster urged me into a chair of the temporary reception, looking a little haggard.

Whatever the penalty was, it was a consequence of my actions... Would it be serious?

"...Just so you know, there's no penalty for you. So you don't need to look so prepared for the worst."

"You mean I'm being acquitted?"

"You considered the safety of the kids being picked on and determined it was too dangerous to leave them and call for help, no? In reality, the kids only got away unharmed thanks to you. The testimonies the six of them gave to the reception matched yours. As for Sacchi and the others, well... You were a little over the top with the restraints, but it can pass if you consider it was for their own safety. Your tardiness was excused for the legitimate reason of helping others. And so, you have no blame in any of this! It's not like you want to take a penalty for fun, right?"

That was true, but why was the guildmaster so worn out then?

"Ah, and also... About Sacchi. This is another one of the reasons why you're not to blame... They weren't to be trusted."

"You mean their claims were inconsistent?"

"Even before that, up until last year they were a gang of ruffians."

"Up until last year?"

I felt there was a deeper meaning to that.

"You wouldn't be able to tell now, but Sacchi used to be an earnest and skilled leader in the past."

I couldn't picture it at all, but as I listened silently to the continuation, I learned that Sacchi's behavior started after he became C rank.

"It's quite a wall for adventurers to advance from rank C to B, with most never making it past C. As the standstill continued, Sacchi gradually lost his will."

In order to advance ranks, his demands of his friends grew higher, and with alcohol and in-fighting thrown in, he went through quite a rough period.

"Then he suddenly grouped up with new adventurers. And not those of the good sort. Ever since, he had been hiding his bad behavior... until today. The guys that caused nothing but problems stopped causing problems, and they seemed to be getting stronger and achieving more steady results... I doubted it at first, but I gradually began to believe Sacchi had turned over a new leaf and was helping the youths grow. Well, it turned out he just got better at hiding it... It's a shame."

Did he feel like he was betrayed by someone he trusted? ...Or nearly trusted, I should say?

If he hadn't believed in Sacchi, he wouldn't have felt sad — even if he doubted them at first, watching over them for a long time would cause lingering attachments. His own expectations had grown, and by the time he noticed it, there was nothing but loss. It was something that repeatedly happened, and was quite hard to get used to.

"...What's that strangely warm look for?"

One day, resignation will come first and make things easier.

I didn't say it out loud, but it showed in my eyes.

"I feel like you're trying to encourage me, but my fatigue is due to you as well, you know? ...If any trouble happens while you're on the job, I have to report it to the duke. My next report's not gonna be fun..."

Ah, now he's worried about the unreasonable demands of those in power. I guess the guildmaster had many worries too. The duke's family was concerned with everything to do with me, after all.

They weren't the type of people to make demands over small things like this, but I could understand the concern.

"You're not even an adult yet... Just what happened in your past?"

I could feel clear pity in his gaze.

"Anyway, discussion with the duke aside, the guild and myself have determined there are no issues involving you. That's all I had to say, you can leave now... If there's anything you're unhappy with, reflect upon it yourself."

"Thank you."

With that wrapped up, I left.

■　■　■

News of what happened had spread through the square while everyone was waiting for the carriages, prompting many adventurers to let me cut in line, figuring I was tired. Thanks to that, I was able to get on a carriage early and reflect on the afternoon.

I didn't have a shred of regret about defeating Sacchi and his gang, but before everything went down I had felt a great sense of irritation. While there was a necessity to my actions, had I not thrown my fist out of anger? Even when I thought about it, I didn't know.

In other words, I couldn't deny it outright.

Am I a child? No. I'm a 42-year-old man in a child's body. A rational adult.

Did I possess rationality? ...I wouldn't say I had none, but there was a chance I could be provoked into a rampage.

Would I punch anyone that bothered me? Would I punch anyone I disliked? ...If so, that would make me no different to those unruly adventurers.

I had plenty of skill and strength, but there seemed to be a problem with my mentality.

...Thinking back on it now, I haven't changed since I came to this world. I secluded myself in a forest, avoided social interactions like my past life, and lived like that. Then I met Reinhart and his family.

If I hadn't met them, I may have extended my stay in the forest forever. Ever since meeting them, I've done nothing but rely on them. They prepared my accommodation and food, welcoming me warmly... Am I being spoiled?

Looking back on everything that happened since coming to this world... I avoided everything I disliked, never suffered hardship, and was spoiled by the kindness of the duke's family... This wouldn't do. At this rate, I'd become a terrible person. All the battle capabilities I had over normal people just made it worse.

I was grateful to the duke's family, but I needed to leave them for a bit. I needed to train myself over from the start. It would do no good for me to continue being cared for by them... I needed independence.

Until now, I had spent much time thinking about how I could ever thank them enough, but even I considered it shameless for someone still relying on them for food and shelter to think about paying them back.

I spent a long time pondering over it on the way back to town, reaching a conclusion by the time I arrived at the inn.

∽ **Chapter 2 Episode 13** ∽
Report

After reaching the inn, I visited the room where the duke's family was staying.

Araune immediately welcomed me, leading me to the table where the four family members were seated.

"Welcome back, Ryoma."

"Welcome back."

"Good to have you back. I heard today was quite an ordeal."

"You shouldn't push yourself too hard."

It seemed like they had already received word of what happened today.

"Thank you, everyone… There's something I would like to tell you all."

The words following my thanks made their expressions stiffen.

"What is it? Tell us."

"Did something happen, Ryoma?"

Reinhart urged me to continue with a serious expression while Eliaria looked at me in worry.

"I've decided on what I want to do in the future. I've been greatly indebted to you all… but I'd like to leave you for my own independence."

The moment I said that, Eliaria shot up from her seat and approached me. The other three remained in their chairs.

"Why are you saying this out of the blue?!"

"At this rate, I'll continue to be spoiled by everyone and become a useless person. In the past two weeks, you have all treated me with so much kindness, I've started to take it for granted. I wish to gain my independence to retrain myself."

"If you want to retrain yourself, why don't you come along with us? We have many people who can act as your instructor..."

"Being with you all makes me behave like a spoiled child. That is why I want to distance myself for a bit."

That was when Elise asked, "When you say a bit, you mean it won't be forever, right?"

"Yes. I'm not leaving because I dislike you all, or anything like that. That is why I hope you'll be willing to see me again, after I am content with my training."

"But of course we would! You know you can act spoiled with us, right? You're still 11 years old, a perfectly normal age to be living with your parents. As long as you wish for it, you're welcome back anytime!"

"Mother! Aren't you going to stop him?"

"Elia, it's not as though you'll never see Ryoma again. Just like how you'll go to school, Ryoma wants to study on his own too. Even though I personally don't think it's necessary. I think what you need is to be spoiled *more*."

"Now, now, Elise. We already agreed, remember?"

"I am aware. That's why I'm not opposing it. I was just stating my opinion."

Already agreed? To what?

"Umm... what did you agree on?"

It was Reinbach and Sebas who answered that question.

"The truth is, we had already predicted you would say such a thing one day when we first arrived in this village. I have lived a long life, after all. Colleagues, subordinates, enemies. Though their positions varied, I've seen many people like you before. We won't stop you. However, you mustn't push yourself too hard. Even if you work hard, if you don't rest properly, you'll put all that hard work to waste."

"Master Ryoma may feel as if he was acting spoiled, but we don't see it that way. While the ducal family has offered the food and shelter for the journey until now, that is all. Master Ryoma, you were the one to register at the guild of an unfamiliar town and take on the jobs, devoting all your efforts to them. As though it was the natural thing to do… That is why we thought this topic would come up one day. Although it was a lot earlier than expected."

Reinhart continued from Sebas's words.

"When I look at you, I'm sometimes reminded of a close friend of mine. Though you have a completely opposite personality. You're serious where he's frivolous. He always tries to push anything bothersome onto his subordinates and others around him, then slack off from his own work… Although we don't want you to go that far either, you need something more like that in yourself. Take frequent breaks and rely on others, just like how Sebas and Father said. Good things will come from that too. That's how my friend is doing well, even now."

…I really was grateful for all their words of advice. I hadn't realized that they considered everything this far.

Before I knew it, tears were spilling from my eyes.

"Thank you… so much."

"Don't worry about it. Instead, we'd like you to promise us a few things. First, you can distance yourself all you want, but you must return to us. The world is a dangerous place, even more so as an adventurer. I'm sure you know that already, but we want to see you again, alive. You can come and show us your face from time to time."

"The second is to write to us regularly, and tell us if anything important happens. If we see you being reckless, we'll send a letter of warning back."

"Or I will pay Master Ryoma a visit myself with my space magic."

"And third, that you won't hesitate to rely on us if you need something! This one is a must! We know that your current knowledge, magic, and combat skills are more than enough. You're skilled enough to be employed, so there's always the option of working for us too."

I didn't know what else to say anymore... I felt nothing but pure gratitude. My weak vocabulary range was troublesome at times like this...

"Ryoma."

I turned to look at Eliaria. She looked straight back at me and said,

"Until now, I haven't had many opportunities to do things with someone else. That's why I'm a little sad... But if it's what you've decided, then I respect that. However!"

The young lady pointed her finger at me and declared, "I'm going to set a condition on that!"

"...Condition?"

"In addition to the three conditions from Father, Grandfather, and Mother. We have to meet again in three years, then again in six years' time."

"Three and six years... but why then?"

"I believe I've told you before, but I'm going to the academy in the capital this year. I'll graduate in six years' time, but I get an extended vacation at the halfway mark, three years in. That's why I want to meet again then. In that time, I'll work hard at studying, learn lots of magic, and grow."

I see, so that's what she meant.

"I understand."

"Good. If you become so absorbed with something and forget... I won't forgive you!" She said, giving me a narrow-eyed glare. It was true that I lost track of time when I got obsessed with something...

"I'll do my best to remember."

"You're supposed to say you definitely won't forget! Hmph..."

Eliaria let out an exasperated noise. Then, Reinhart asked me with a laugh, "Hahaha, I'm sure it'll be fine. By the way, Ryoma. Have you decided what you'll do?"

"I have my slimes, so I think I'll live in the outskirts of this town. Then I'll live here as an adventurer and train myself while interacting with others."

"I see... In that case, could I ask you for one thing?"

"What is it? I'd be happy to help."

"I'd like to ask you to manage the mines that you're currently exterminating monsters at. It was only abandoned for a year, yet more monster nests were formed than expected... Having monster nests so close to town is most unfavorable. That's why I want you to patrol them regularly and subjugate the monster nests. If it's too much for one person, then put up a job through the guild. I considered sealing the exit, but cave mantises can dig holes with their forelegs to create nests so there's not much point."

"If that's all you need, then I can do it."

"Thank you. In return, you can use the mines however you please. You should be fine to fire magic and train there without disturbing others."

"That would be..."

That would be perfect for me! I'd have a place to build a house a decent distance from town and the lack of people around would make it perfect for training, letting my slimes move about freely, and making ingots. It was worth more than money could buy, to me.

"This is an official trade. There are dangerous species of monsters out there. If one made a nest in the mines and multiplied, it'd be a danger to the nearby town. Normally the public office would send an employee to check on the state of things and hire someone to take care of it, but... It seems like the office in this town didn't do any managing, so I'm hiring someone skilled that I trust instead. While a separate reward would normally be paid to the manager, we can just let you use the place however you like, since it has no value to us or this town. No hassle, no expense."

...While that certainly sounded possible, I could tell it was a reason given retroactively. After all, the public office employees that had abandoned their work had been punished. They should all be doing their duties properly under the new management right now.

Reinhart seemed to notice me thinking such things, as he said with a strained smile, "Goodness, you really are far too serious... Don't let the small things bother you. How about we do it this way: if you make ingots while you're there, we'll be benefiting too. Just don't push yourself too hard making them."

"...I understand. I'll do my best to fulfill my duty!"

I'd set a monthly quota and visit Serge's store every month. If I didn't do that much, it wouldn't be an equal trade.

"No, you don't need to be that enthusiastic about it..."

"Also, we want you to stay in this inn for the duration that we're in town."

"But that's..."

"I don't want to hear any buts. I was expecting to travel together with you a little longer. But you've decided to go off and grow up so fast on your own. That's why I've decided on this!"

"It will only be for another one or two months at most. You can always retrain yourself after. That should be perfect for someone who likes to work too hard like you."

…If I didn't reject them here, I'd continue to—

"We won't continue to spoil you, Master Ryoma."

Sebas read my mind?!

"Ryoma. All your thoughts are showing on your face."

"Your face is terribly easy to read, after all."

Is it really that obvious?

"Anyway! You will be staying with us in this inn while we're in town! Got it?"

"But…"

"I said, got it?"

"But…"

"You've got it, right?! Right?!"

Elise clearly wouldn't listen to any answer other than a yes… Fine… But was my will always this weak…? Though I was extremely grateful for the offer…

"I got it, I'll continue being spoiled by everyone's kindness until you leave town."

"Good! That's a relief."

In the end, I couldn't refuse.

I didn't want to dismiss their kindness, and in the end, I was happier having people who cared about me.

I thanked everyone and returned to my room.

⟿ Chapter 2 Episode 14 ⟿
Monster Subjugation at the Mines, Day 2

Continuing on from yesterday, today was another monster subjugation day.

I had said I wanted to be independent last night, so I wanted to do what I could right now.

First, I had to secure the basic living necessities. Clothes I could always buy in town, and now I had the mines, so accommodation was fine too. For food, I'd find a new hunting ground and buy whatever I was missing. But in order to buy food, I needed money.

At present, I had the 700 small golds from that bandit bounty, as well as 40 medium golds from the bandits belongings. I also had the money I had made working until now, so I was fine for the time being. If anything, it was a frivolous amount of money, but of course it would vanish if I used it thoughtlessly.

Well, if I took the guild's 30 pit toilet cleaning jobs at 3 medium silvers, that would be 3000 sutes, more than enough to live off for 30 days. I would make more than enough by selling iron ingots and waterproof fabric to Serge on top of that. That's why I wasn't troubled for money, but to say I was living easy wasn't quite right either…

Imagining a future with a life of just this was depressing. Especially since the toilet cleaning could be left to the scavenger slimes now, leaving me nothing to do. If I lived comfortably with that as my source of income, then I would have left the duke's family for nothing.

Should I look for other sources of income outside of being an adventurer? Hmm... There could be something to cause me to cease being an adventurer one day, too.

I had lived the three years between coming to this world and meeting Reinhart without spending a single sute, so at worst, I only needed to make as much as I needed to live. If I were to treat the fortune I had right now as an emergency fund... 100 sute a day. I wanted to save for retirement, but if I could make at least that much a day, it should be plenty.

"Ryoma. Hey, you listening?"

Oops, my bad. I was lost in my thoughts...

"Sorry, I was thinking. What did you say?"

"Thinking in the middle of a battle would be dangerous... Is what I would like to say, but..."

"You're defeating the monsters easily without even thinking about it..."

"You haven't left any for us."

"Ah, I'm sorry. My body was moving unconsciously..."

"That's fine, but could you stop muttering to yourself while you're calmly ending one monster after another, nya? It's a little scary to watch."

"I apologize for that..."

I guess I was thinking out loud...

"Based on your mutterings, you're being troubled by money? Something about living costs?"

"Actually..."

"Everyone!! Gather at the mine entrance!!"

Just as I was about to explain the circumstances, a man came rushing over in a huge panic. Did something urgent happen?

"What happened?!"

"A goblin village was established in one of the mineshafts. And it's a fairly large one, too. Thankfully no one was killed, but several G rankers were injured."

"A goblin village, huh? What a pain. If we don't put a stop to it quickly, their numbers will increase very quickly."

"I still have to warn the others, so please head to the entrance first!"

The man said as he ran off.

■　■　■

A large number of adventurers had already gathered at the mine entrance. After waiting for a short while, the guildmaster appeared on the podium that was prepared.

"I'm sure most of you have heard already, but I'll explain once more! Just now, we found a mineshaft with goblins living inside, leading to a village nearby! Thus, we will now begin a goblin extermination! The scale will be medium sized! There are roughly 500 goblins or so! Parties will be formed out of D-rank adventurers and above, to keep damage to a minimum! Gather in your ranks and follow any further orders!!"

The guildmaster cut off there and called me out.

"Also… Ryoma, are you there?"

"I'm over here."

"You're currently F rank, but your abilities are above E rank. You've also fulfilled the conditions to advance to E rank with the job request this time. It's a little early, but you'll be participating as an E ranker this time."

"I understand."

"Anyone with a problem with that?"

No one objected to the guildmaster's words. The events of yesterday must have still been fresh in their minds.

"All right, everyone get ready! Anyone lacking supplies or necessities, come to me! I'll help prepare whatever I can! Once you've prepared, gather in your respective ranks and beat the plan into your heads!"

Once we gathered in our ranks and a woman named Ploria was selected as the E-rank leader, we began our meeting with her in charge.

"I will now explain the outline of the plan this time... Our job is to take the F- and G-rank adventurers along and prevent the goblins from running away, defeating any that are missed by the others."

She used a large map to explain the plan.

"First, the problematic mineshaft and village will be flanked on all sides by A-, B-, C-, and D-ranked adventurers before charging in. They'll exterminate most of the goblins, but there will most likely be some missed due to the large numbers. That is where we'll come in, waiting by the areas where the encirclement is deliberately weaker to drive them in a single direction and finish them off. Furthermore, we'll have the inexperienced F- and G-ranked adventurers with us. Because of that, we'll want to be as safe as possible in our actions. If you have a suggestion towards how to accomplish that, I ask that you raise your hand."

Several people raised their hands at that and gave their suggestions. Following them, I also offered the method I used in the forest.

"Ryoma, was it. Do you have something?"

"Yes, a method to deal with many goblins at once. If we use earth magic to dig a deep hole between the nest and our location, I can put my acid slime familiars inside. Then..."

From my Item Box, I took out a long pole with a knife attached at the end like a scythe.

"We can use weapons like these to drop the goblins into the hole, and let the acid do the rest. Goblins in the distance can be dealt with through magic or arrows. With this method, the goblins are powerless once they've fallen in. Not many can climb out, and those that try can be pushed back in with spears or other weapons. We have to keep an eye out for goblin archers and mages, but otherwise even inexperienced people can fight safely."

"I see... and the slimes needed to accomplish that would be..."

"I can prepare them all."

The others seemed to deem it a suggestion worth considering. They had questions about it, so we worked out the details as I answered them until we ultimately decided to go with a plan based on my idea.

"Now, please move to your positions quickly."

With that quiet order, we all began the task we were assigned.

My role was to take several adventurers who could use earth magic to the ambush point first and dig a hole.

"Looking at it like this, it's a lot deeper than expected."

"The goblins shouldn't be able to climb out of this."

The designated location had cliffs on both sides of the path like a valley, so we'd have visibility if they tried to run to the sides. There, we would dig a pit 4 meters long, 50 meters wide, and 3 meters deep to narrow their escape.

"*Create Block!*"

"That spell is amazing."

"It's a combination of Rock and Break Rock! It's very efficient."

"Can I try it too?"

"Of course!"

With an emphasis on efficiency, I occasionally taught magic as we began digging a pit with holes scattered about the bottom, leading to small caverns. By hiding the core of the acid slimes, the danger of them being knocked into goblin bodies and weapons would be reduced. Acid slimes could extend their bodies and expel acid through the holes, melting the goblins that fell in.

Once the hole was prepared, simply placing the acid slimes in them was enough to create a highly acidic pool of digestive fluids.

"Hey, can I throw this in as a test?"

"I want to see the effect."

"Sure."

With that, the adventurer threw a small rat's corpse into the pool.

The skin of the corpse immediately began to disintegrate until the bone was exposed before sinking out of sight.

"...Nasty..."

"Were acid slimes always this dangerous...?"

"Normally if they spit on you, you'd get away with just your skin burned off. But if you get submerged like this with no escape, you'll eventually dissolve down to your bones. Melted prey becomes nutrients that make it easier to produce more digestive fluids, so if the plan goes well the volume will steadily increase as time passes. Though once it reaches a certain point I'll give them the order to stop."

"I never want to fall in that..."

"Excuse me! Where should I place the supplies?"

Oh, it looks like the separate party with the supplies had arrived. They had gathered long sticks from the nearby trees and piles of bladed forelegs from the cave mantises defeated by adventurers from yesterday and today.

While the cave mantises' blades weren't sharp, they were durable and well-suited for tripping up and striking goblins, so they had been put forth as a suggestion. I gave an order to my sticky slimes to produce a hardening solution to attach the blades to the sticks.

On top of that, I used the earth we dug up from the pit to create a handrail to the side of the hole so that we didn't fall in accidentally. I also created some platforms for archers and magicians to gain a height advantage and make it easier for them to fire long distance, thus concluding our preparations.

Since the platform was eye-catching, I put up some physical damage barriers with barrier magic. The problem with these barriers was how magic would fly right past, so I made sure to warn everyone of that.

With that reported to the leader, my job was done.

"Final checks! F- and G-rank adventurers, stay by the pit and use the scythes to deal with goblins, E-rank adventurers stay on both sides of the pit for close combat, driving them safely towards the pit while making sure the F and G rankers are safe. Archers and magicians prioritize any goblin archers and mages as soon as they're spotted."

Acknowledgments of the leader's orders could be heard from every direction.

"And now, everyone should rest up until the plan commences."

With everything prepared, all that was left was to wait for the time to come. Other than the adventurers placed on watch, everyone began to rest. However, I was left free just like yesterday. I guess I could check over my slimes and weapons once more.

"Excuse me! Do you have a moment right now?!"

"Huh?"

I turned around to look at who suddenly called...

"Ah, I remember you guys from yesterday..."

And saw the six kids standing there.

⇌ Chapter 2 Episode 15 ⇌
Inquiry

I see. 'F- and G-rank adventurers' would include them as well.

"Yes! Thank you for yesterday!"

"Thank you for yesterday!"

The others echoed the words of the girl who spoke first, bowing their heads and attracting the curious eyes of people around us. I suppose there was no point in telling them not to look. Since my surroundings were dominated by countless slimes on standby to assist with the job, their presence alone was quite eye-catching.

"Umm, what's this about…?"

Their attitudes were quite different to yesterday, though I had an idea why.

"We wanted to thank you for saving us and apologize for our attitude yesterday."

"Well, thank you for that. I'm glad you were safe too. I'm Ryoma Takebayashi, a human. As you can see, these are my slime familiars."

This was my third time meeting these kids, but I still didn't know their names. I introduced myself since they came to thank me, but it caused them to stiffen nervously as they introduced themselves back.

And to my surprise, they were…

A monkey beastkin named Beck, aged 13.

A dog beastkin named Ruth, aged 12.

An ape beastkin named Wist, aged 11.

…Those were the boys, and as for the girls…

A half-elf named Martha, aged 12.

A half-dwarf named Finia, aged 12.

And a dog beastkin named Rumille, aged 12.

I had assumed they were two beastkin people and four humans, but I was wrong.

The two halflings were completely human in appearance, and the ape and monkey beastkin were also misleading!

For the record, Beck was the shortest one that spoke the most. Unfortunately, his height and rude tone had made him seem like nothing more than an arrogant child, but he was actually the eldest and trying to act as the leader.

Also, the ape beastkin Wist was actually the youngest, despite being the biggest. I had assumed he was the oldest.

"The adults said my height was an issue with my species…"

His personality was also the picture of timidness. I asked about the different impression I had of him yesterday when he was cornered against the wall, and he said it was because he squeezed out all his willpower while working so that the other adventurers wouldn't look down on him. He did seem intimidating for his age when he was standing silently, though.

An ape beastkin and monkey beastkin. Now that I knew that, I could see the resemblance to a gorilla and golden snub-nosed monkey when I looked at them… especially in their hair colors. I didn't say it out loud to be polite, but now I couldn't see them as anything but that.

But that aside…

They were still children, but they all excelled in their respective species traits of physical abilities and magic energy.

Ruth and Rumille had the dog beastkin characteristics of a sharp nose and good physical balance, while the half-elf Martha specialized in magic. The monkey beastkin Beck could nimbly scale any tree with ease, while the ape beastkin Wist and half-dwarf Finia had extraordinary strength for children, which they showed me.

It was interesting to compare the traits between species. But…

"That's amazing. I can tell you excel in physical abilities."

"It's not amazing…"

"W-We lost against someone our own age for the first time, bro."

"I saw… The two of you lost, but you have just as much strength as an adult adventurer. We became adventurers to make use of our advantages and earn a living. But even though we can move better than adults, adults make more money. That's why when we saw you, who looked even younger than us, we said those things. We're really sorry, Ryoma."

While having better physical abilities was certainly an advantage, it didn't mean they could do jobs any better. Even in a single hunt, there were many things to do like finding your target prey, knowing where to aim for, and choosing how to do it. They had yet to learn such techniques. They lacked the experience.

"Like I said before, I don't mind the words you said to me. But there are a few things I'm curious about."

"Ask us anything. We don't have anything to hide anyway."

In that case, I would do just that.

"I was feeding my slimes when my metal slime rolled away and I happened to hear the commotion while I was picking it up. But why were you there in the first place?"

They were probably taken there by the men, but it was still lunch at that time. If they were in the square, they could have sought help — or so I thought, when their expressions fell.

"We couldn't carry everything your squad let us have in one go."

"We didn't have enough bags..."

Finia added to Beck's explanation. Now that they mentioned it, there was a fair bit more than they could have possibly carried at once. They probably couldn't use the space magic Item Box either.

"So they picked a fight with you when you were on your way to get it?"

"I think they would have done so at some point eventually, even without that. It was the second time yesterday they picked on us too."

When I asked Rumille for more details, the six kids looked a little frustrated.

"Last week the six of us went into the forest in the north for a herb-gathering job, but there were five of them there doing another job. When we got close, they yelled at us saying we made their prey run away. They've probably had their eyes on us ever since."

"Were you okay?"

"We were the ones at fault back then, so it didn't end up as a fight. They didn't ask for anything as unreasonable as yesterday, so we just paid up. That man named Sacchi coincidentally passed by and told how much the prey that got away would have been worth, and how much the penalty fees for the job would be... We didn't know he was their friend. Now that we look back on it, they had probably planned it from the start."

So he ripped them off by pretending to be the mediator, huh?

"But if they split it amongst such a large group of people, it couldn't have been worth much..."

"Yesterday they said... even our low income was enough to fund drinks for one night..."

Were they not particular over the amount of money, or were they collecting from other people too? Well, the guild would investigate that. More importantly, though.

"Then, my next question... Based on what I've heard until now, you guys can hunt to an extent too."

At the very least, I saw them defeat cave bats and small rats. The six of them nodded at my words.

"Then why did you try to steal other people's kills?"

"...We thought we could make more money that way."

"We started off the monster subjugation like everyone else, but it took time. Then we saw the adult adventurers throw away their kills, saying they couldn't be bothered... We're truly sorry."

Martha bowed her head once more, but that wasn't what I wanted to hear.

"Sorry, I worded my question badly. I wanted to ask why you're in such desperate need for money. Was it really difficult to live on what you had, or was there another reason?"

"Our living conditions are poor, but it was to pay the resident tax."

Unexpected words came from Ruth's mouth.

"Resident tax. Just to confirm, that's tax you pay to the town you live in, right?"

"What else could it be? You have to pay the fees to live in town."

Resident tax in this world not only went to maintenance of outer walls and payment of guards, but gave you the right to be protected from monsters and bandits. I had never paid it since I lived in the forest outside the walls, but living within the walls created the duty to pay up. Their words were correct.

But, sorry guys. I just couldn't believe you were paying the tax properly.

"Sorry, I'm not too familiar with resident tax. Is the tax in Gimul really that high?"

"The resident tax we pay in Gimul is 400 sutes per person. I've never lived in another town before so I don't know if it's expensive, but we have to pay anyway. Because if we don't pay up, we can't live in town."

For six people, that was 2400 sutes. I could pay that much immediately, but it must have been a fortune to people barely making a living.

"So how did you pay it up until now?"

I didn't know if they had parents, but if they lived in the town before they must have paid it somehow.

"We earned it by cleaning toilets."

"...Could that be the pit toilets?"

"You've heard of them? We got money from the public office for cleaning them. But the amount gradually decreased and the adults in the slums told us to stop, since it would only make us sick. That's why we became adventurers."

"Ah, I see..."

What was this feeling of exhaustion, I wonder. I hadn't been mad with them to begin with, but the more I listened, the less energy I had to be angry.

"...Hey, did I say something bad?"

"I-I don't know... Is he m-mad...?"

Ah, it seemed like I was worrying them.

"I'm not mad, don't worry. Err... Regarding the resident tax, are there any assistance programs to help?"

As far as I was aware, no one should be kicked out immediately if they couldn't pay the resident tax...

"I heard there were ways you could work in the mines as well."

"Assistance programs? ...If you mean what happens when we can't pay, then I've heard you can write it off by working... But that's the job of the people who stopped paying us in the first place, y'know? We couldn't trust them, and we weren't the only ones troubled by the lack of work with the toilet cleaning gone, so we could have been excluded from that work. Also, the mines don't hire children. Someone decided that a long time ago. No matter how much stamina we have, so many adults are also looking for jobs, so they refuse to break their customs and end up turning us away."

The effects of that pit toilet incident reached all the way here...

"For now, I've asked everything I wanted to know. Thanks."

"R-Right."

The six of them looked unsettled by the sudden gratitude, but I brushed it off and told them that the Adventurer's Guild was currently managing cleaning of the pit toilets. They listened intently when I informed them that the pay wouldn't be messed with anymore. It seemed like they were willing to work seriously.

In the future, I should only pick up the toilet jobs when my scavenger slimes were low on food.

∾ **Chapter 2 Episode 16** ∾
Group Battle

After my reconciliation (or an unreasonable facsimile thereof) with Beck's party, and asking them to spread the news about the pit toilets, it was time for the plan to commence.

"Is everyone in position? The enemies may appear immediately! Be careful!"

Everyone was fired up at Ploria's words, a tension hovering over the area.

I was also on high alert with my bow in hand, and ten minutes later the first goblin appeared.

"They're here! Three from the front! More following behind!"

"Got it!"

Beck reported the discovery first from the top of the tree he had climbed, to which everyone around us responded. The goblins had noticed us too, but they charged at us in a straight line. They weren't very smart creatures to begin with.

Out of the three goblins, one of them didn't notice the pit and fell in on its own. The second one noticed and came to a stop, but the long scythe-wielding adventurers dragged it into the pit, while the third one tried to leap over it but couldn't reach the other side.

The goblins screamed as their skin was melted by the acid, but their cries of suffering quieted in a few seconds. The following goblins continued to meet the same fate.

Occasionally a goblin archer or goblin mage would appear and remain at a distance, but those were taken care of by adventurers with bows and magic.

For the record, all the arrows we were using had been coated with poison from poison slimes. Since the enemies were put to an end even with a light injury, we were yet to suffer any damage through arrows and magic.

Archers were identifiable immediately by their bows, and goblin mages could be detected with the magic detection skill, and it wasn't as though they were any good at using them either. They were so slow, there was plenty of time to detect their magic energy before firing an attack.

The conditions for us were far superior. But there were many more than we expected in numbers... There were no injuries yet, but I had never seen so many before. We'd soon surpass 500, the number that was predicted to be the nest total. Had something happened in the main fight?

The acid slimes were gradually falling behind in their consumption, and goblin corpses were beginning to build up in the pit.

It wasn't enough to panic yet, but at this rate... The adventurers around me had noticed too and reacted in confusion.

"Isn't this strange?!"

"Indeed, there's far more than there should be."

"At this rate I'm going to run out of arrows!"

"I only have a few arrows left too!"

"You there! Don't let your arrows go to waste!"

"Hah... Hah... Why are there so many goblins... How long will they keep coming for?!"

Goblins were weak and only as tall as a human child, but they had the intellect to use weapons. And most importantly, they could reproduce and multiply their numbers rapidly. If you underestimated them for being weak, you'd be swallowed up in no time at all.

They ate both human and animal meat. Though they had similar bodies to humans, there was no friendship to be had there.

Even if their skills were poor, having that many of them swing around bladed tools was dangerous and more than any person could handle alone. Based on our meeting earlier, there were over 100 people on our side too, but most of them were F and G rank. They could only barely take on a goblin one-on-one, at most. There was no way they would be allowed forward, where things could get messy.

Thus, only E-rank adventurers could be at the front line, out of necessity. But we didn't have enough in numbers. E rankers were still practically newbies themselves, having trained enough to have some form of ability.

Furthermore, not every E ranker was capable of close combat. There were those who used magic and bows, and others who specialized in healing magic. That's why there were only 28 people in charge of close-ranged combat. I could already see fatigue in them from holding the frontline until now. Several had been injured and treated with magic before returning to the battle. It was clear they would reach their limit at this rate.

Our plans could have covered a large number of running goblins, but there were just way more than expected. It was a small mercy that the goblins weren't streaming out like an avalanche, making it somewhat manageable...

This was bad... The frontline was finally running low on steam.

"Ploria, could my slimes and I take over the frontlines for a bit? It looks like the battle will be a long one, so the frontline can rest in that time."

"Ryoma… the guildmaster said you were above E but… All right, can I count on you? Buy us as much time as possible, without pushing yourself too hard."

When I suggested the swap in positions to the commanding leader, she answered within seconds.

"Understood."

"Frontliners on both sides! Ryoma and his slimes will be joining you! Swap over and rest as much as possible!"

I called over all the sticky slimes, poison slimes, and scavenger slimes that had been waiting at the back and sent them to the front lines on both sides. Then I jumped down from my high platform and leaped over the pit before giving my orders to the slimes.

"Show me the results of your training up until now against the goblins!"

At that moment, all the slimes started quivering in a display of enthusiasm. Each one extended a feeler towards the goblins.

One sticky slime picked up a stick discarded by a goblin and began handling it nimbly. As a group, they beat the goblins and sent them rolling, or otherwise used sticky solution to halt their movements.

A poison slime picked up a shabby spear used by the goblins and spat poison over the tip.

The scavenger slimes slipped under the feet of the goblins and tripped them up with their feelers. Or they would allow themselves to be stepped on before rolling their bodies out to trip them, then cover the faces of the fallen goblins.

Lacking in pure strength, they couldn't punch the goblins to death, but fighting one-on-one they could hold their own. The slimes acted as a group, attacking the goblins in their own ways, putting an end to them.

Especially the poison slimes, whose secretions proved a powerful and especially effective weapon.

It looked like I could leave this to them.

Beside them, I drew my two daggers.

I was probably seen as a target. I closed the distance to an approaching goblin and stabbed it through the heart.

Withdrawing my dagger, I slashed the throat of another goblin passing.

"Gukeeh?!"

"Gowah!"

"Gweeh!!"

A goblin tried to raise its sword in a completely open stance, so I slashed the tendons in its wrists and kicked it down. The rest the slimes could handle.

"Geeeeh."

I evaded the goblin's spear coming from behind and circled around. When my dagger pierced its medulla oblongata, it collapsed like a puppet cut from its strings.

One of the traits of a goblin was how similar in shape it was to a human, but that applied to both their appearance and their organs. They were sturdier than humans, but they could be finished off in a single blow if their vitals were struck with accuracy, and rendered immobile by cutting their wrists and carotid arteries.

At the very least, the goblins I had fought until now died like that. Just like now. So it shouldn't be a problem to deal with it as I have until now.

Every time I killed one, blood would spurt everywhere as the goblins screamed, but I ignored them all and single-mindedly continued to hack away at them.

However, they really kept on coming. Where were they hiding such numbers?

The goblins were still steadily coming, and combat power-wise we were starting to struggle. Since we had the advantage of numbers we had a little more leeway now, so I ordered the slimes that weren't fighting to collect arrows.

"Hold on... hah... Isn't that kid... way too strong? ...We were struggling... so much..."

"We've been saved..."

"It looks like we can leave it to that kid for now... We'll rest up as much as we can while he buys us time! Then we'll swap over!"

"Right!!!"

"Huh, are those really slimes?"

"Those slimes... they're good at using spears. Even better than me..."

"They're good... wait, why are slimes using weapons?!"

"So many weird things are happening, but at least we're saved... Hmm? An arrow?"

"Oh?! Bow team! The slimes have gathered the arrows! Hey you, move it! Let the slimes pass!"

I could hear the voices of the frontline, so it seemed like they were resting properly. That aside, I guess it was rare for slimes to use weapons, huh... Or rather, were they really so carefree as to worry about that right now?

Just as I thought that, I felt more magical energy. Another goblin mage, huh?

I returned my right dagger to its sheath and took out throwing knives instead, finishing it off that way. The slimes and I continued doing that until the others had recovered their stamina.

⇜ Chapter 2 Episode 17 ⇝
Fight Over, Fight Ongoing

The battle continued with several turns resting and healing the injured, until the goblins finally stopped coming at over the 2000 mark.

Thanks to the efforts of the healers and healing slimes, there were no serious injuries among the adventurers, but there were so many goblin corpses along the front line that there was no space to stand.

Then suddenly, four men appeared through space magic.

"What's the status here, everyone?!"

"Sorry we took so long! What is the situation?"

"It looks like everything's okay? …Wow, there's a ton of corpses here too."

"Leipin, Asagi, Gordon, Sher. You came for us."

They must have had a hard-fought battle themselves… Other than Leipin the magician, everyone was covered in blood splatters.

"Oh! You're safe, Ryoma!"

"It seems like you've been through a lot yourself. There's blood all over you."

"We're not ones to talk, though."

"That's true. But what was with those numbers? Over 2000 goblins came this way. Though judging by your appearances, you had to deal with quite a few on your end too…"

"Indeed, we owe you an explanation about that."

"Erm, who's the person in charge here? We'd like to ask about the situation here."

"That'd be me!"

Ploria ran up to the four men and explained the situation until now.

"...I see. So that's how it went."

"Yes. We were able to endure it thanks to Ryoma and his slimes. Our team would have been wiped out otherwise."

"With this many numbers... it's a miracle you all survived practically unharmed."

"At any rate, it's great that everyone's safe."

"Umm, how did things go in the main army?"

"For now, the situation has come to an end. However..."

"While there were no deaths, there were some serious injuries. Their numbers were far beyond what we expected when scouting, and there was even a goblin king. It had crowds of goblin knights as lackeys."

"There was a goblin king?!"

Ploria's shout stirred our surroundings.

"You lot! The goblin king has been dealt with already, so don't worry!"

Gordon's single statement calmed everyone a bit, before they burst into cheers. As they did, the explanation continued.

"We planned our strategy around a map of the mines, but it seemed like the goblins had dug their own mineshafts and expanded their village. The scouts' probes couldn't reach to the depths of the mineshaft, which actually turned out to be connected to another shaft that wasn't on the map."

"The village we thought we were attacking was ultimately a small piece of a larger whole. Their numbers had grown significantly on the other side, so they continuously streamed from their nesting hole. We only noticed that the real village and boss was on the other side of the shaft some time after we began our attack. Because of that, many goblins fled through a different route and ended up surging through here. We were completely inadequate; forgive us."

"So that's what happened... None of us were severely injured, so we don't have anything in particular to say about that, though... How did a village of that size go unnoticed until now?"

"We believe their numbers grew that large because they never approached the town and stayed hidden in the mineshaft, feeding off other monsters. There were an enormous number of small rat and cave bat remains left behind. And it seems like no one has approached this abandoned mine since last year, so..."

"Because the folks at the public office were negligent. With no more iron being harvested, maintenance of these mines is nothing more than an expense. However..."

Leipin looked around at our surroundings.

"You truly did very well, managing to escape unharmed against this many enemies. If there are no problems here, may I take several of your healers with us? I'd like to get the injured on the other side treated."

"I understand. Anyone with healing magic and enough energy left, gather up!"

Four people including me stepped forward at Ploria's words.

"Hmm... Unfortunately, three is the maximum number of people I can take with space magic. I'd have to ask one of you to make your own way there..."

"In that case, I'll stay back. I've started learning space magic myself recently, so I'll catch up in no time."

"That's good to hear."

"Ah, Leipin. Are you able to take a few more things?"

"As long as they aren't very large."

Hearing that, I called forth my two healing slimes.

"Then please take these two slimes. I can still only teleport myself."

"I understand. But what type are they? These slimes."

"Healing slimes, slimes that can use healing magic."

"Oh ho! So these are healing slimes! I've studied monsters for a long time now, but this is my first time seeing one. All right, I shall take responsibility for these two."

"Thank you so much."

"No problem. We'll be waiting on the other side. *Warp*."

As soon as he said that, Leipin took the three others with him and teleported. I bid farewell to Ploria and the others before setting off too.

"Ploria, I'll be leaving my slimes behind, so please take care of them. You can just leave them alone."

"Leave it to me. Thanks for taking care of the other side."

"Yes. Now then… *Teleport*."

I repeated my short distance teleportation until I reached an isolated location, then used the intermediate spell Warp.

The location I arrived at had many injured people receiving treatment.

"Ryoma! This way."

Leipin was there. I ran over to him and received my two healing slimes from him before I was led to the recovery supervisor and given orders.

The two healing slimes and I were first allocated to those with comparatively lighter wounds. They were all conscious and surprised to be receiving treatment from a slime's healing magic.

Once I finished my work there, I was immediately ordered to assist with the treatment of the more severely wounded patients.

Since I was running low on magic energy, I drank the magic recovery potions I received from Serge the other day as I went about treating patients.

There were only a few people who were wounded to a life-threatening level, but those people were bleeding profusely and being taken care of by several healers with the intermediate healing magic High Heal. The wounds were too big for us to treat, but I helped out all the same, as it would provide temporary relief. I distributed a few of my potions on hand to the other healers as well.

"Guh…"

We had to stop the bleeding as soon as possible. If the magic stopped, the person before me would be closer to death.

The bustling movement here was on par with a battlefield. There was no time to think.

"Huh?!"

As I silently continued giving treatment, someone looking after a different patient to me suddenly yelled out loud.

"What's wrong?! Do you need assistance?!"

The man who was healing the same patient as me shouted back.

"N-No! There's no problem here!"

"The slime assisting us here suddenly used High Heal, so we were surprised!"

…WHAT?! My healing slime?! The healing slime should only have been able to use Heal, though? It's never used anything else before…

When the man heard their answer, he looked to me as though asking if my slimes could really use High Heal.

"I think they only learned it just now. I've never seen them use it before."

"The more help, the better!"

And with that, we returned to healing. Not too long after, a different person looking after another patient also yelled when the other healing slime started using that spell. It was an unexpected development, but it was a success.

Process aside, their treatment efficiency rose dramatically, and with the large number of magic recovery potions I retrieved from my Item Box, we somehow succeeded in healing the patient. He would still need some time before he could get back on his feet, but his life was no longer in danger.

With the urgency of treatment slightly relieved, I appraised the healing slime's skills to find its healing magic skill had risen to level 3. Additionally, when I looked at my own status board, I found I was now level 2.

"I suppose using it that much would raise it... Hmm?"

I was suddenly surrounded by over 10 people, thanking me profusely through my confusion. Apparently we had healed a friend of theirs. They insisted through their tears and crying that their friend would have died if it hadn't been for me, my healing slimes, and my potions.

While I was troubled for a response, the guildmaster wandered over and let me escape with a message to pass to the ambush team. The message was to gather before the mine entrance.

Thanks!

I expressed my gratitude for the guildmaster's actions in my heart, and hurried back to the ambush team.

163

■ ■ ■

Once all the adventurers that could move gathered before the mine entrance.

"Good work today! It was a bigger job than expected, but that means your rewards will increase accordingly!"

The guildmaster announced as he appeared, receiving cheers.

"The minimum reward for this job has been raised to one large silver coin for everyone!"

The cheers grew louder at that. Especially among the G-rank adventurers. One large silver coin was 5000 sutes, enough to live on for 50 days. They had probably never received such a high reward before.

"Anyone with complaints? No? Good! It's still early in the day, but you can all go home after cleaning up the goblin corpses!"

That was when the guildmaster looked at me as though he remembered something.

"That's right, Ryoma!"

"What is it?"

"You said you were buying the bodies of the monsters, but you can have the goblins for free."

"I'm very grateful to receive them, but are you sure I can have them for free?"

"There are no profitable parts to a goblin, after all. Is everyone fine with that?"

There were many adventurers around me that were unaware I was the one buying the monsters and reacted in surprise, but no one objected. There were even people who appreciated the less effort required on their part. Normally they would have been disposed of by incineration, so the fire magicians wouldn't have enjoyed being sought for their fire magic when they were low on energy as it was.

"Then I shall gladly receive them. I'll let the slimes eat their fill as their reward."

But I felt bad for simply taking them, so I'll offer a cleaner slime bath to anyone who wants one later as a service.

The adventurers returned to their posts and I returned to the ambush team too.

I retrieved my acid slimes that had reabsorbed their acid and threw all the goblin corpses into the remaining pit for my sticky and poison slimes to eat their fill. This way, the poison slimes could determine the goblins that had died from poison and eat those, while the sticky slimes ate the rest.

I ordered my scavenger slimes to eat the blood and body parts remaining on the ground, and once they were done there wasn't a trace left.

Wouldn't this be the perfect way to conceal evidence of a crime...? Better make sure it never fell into the wrong hands. Well, I had no intention of giving them to anyone anyway.

...Now, just one job left.

While the slimes had been feeding, I first taught the E, F and G rankers about the abilities of the cleaner slimes and then demonstrated on myself. After I showed them how my body, equipment, and clothes were rid of all dirt and scents, the number of people interested surged. In fact, all of them said they wanted to try it.

After the 11 cleaner slimes had cleaned everyone up, we waited for the slimes in the pit to finish eating before heading to the main team in the goblin's nest.

There were several piles of goblin corpses left around, so we disposed of those and cleaned the equipment and people again. The scavenger slimes once more ate the dirt on the floor and around the goblin's nest.

As with before, the cleaner slime baths were extremely popular due to how difficult it was to wash off goblin blood and scents.

Once everything was disposed of, we were dismissed to return via horse carriage.

My slimes and I rested from a distance as we watched the adventurers do that.

By feeding the goblins to the slimes today, the poison, acid, and cleaner slimes were ready to split again. However, I had no magic energy to form contracts, so I was waiting for that to recover.

To recover as quickly as I could, I was leisurely waiting for the final carriage, rather than scramble to board one as soon as possible.

Time had flown past since I was added to the healing team... I was bushed...

⇌ Chapter 2 Episode 18 ⇋
Return Home

"What are you doing here, Ryoma?"

As I was staring into space with my slimes, Jeff's voice reached my ears. Behind him was the team that had been gathered for the toilet cleaning.

"Aren't you leaving, nya?"

"Thanks for your work today, everyone. Even if I wanted to leave, the crowds at the carriages are a bit... I thought I'd just wait until the last one."

"You too, huh?"

"Does that mean everyone is also...?"

"Everyone's tired today, so we're not in the mood to join that crowd."

"Good grief... Even though we were hired precisely in case something like today happened, it was tough."

"That's for sure. A goblin king on top of a swarm that size... That would normally be a job requiring full preparations. It made me recall that one conversation while I was fighting... the one not to underestimate weak monsters."

"Ah, the tale of how a kingdom was once destroyed under the attack of 100,000 goblins? I recalled that too. Honestly, it was a miracle that no one died today."

Was there really such a tale?

When Gordon wound his thick arm around his neck and grumbled that, Mizelia agreed. Everyone was tired too, huh... Just as I thought that, Sher suddenly asked, "Huh? Ryoma, don't you know about this? It's a pretty famous tale..."

"I don't remember..."

"You must have been the type of kid to read textbooks instead of fairy tales, huh?"

Everyone accepted Jeff's words. My simple lack of knowledge was misunderstood. I was turning into a studious nerd within their minds.

"The efforts of the kingdom's soldiers and adventurers were in vain, as they were pushed back by sheer numbers. We can laugh about it now, but if it weren't for you and your slimes, the ambush team would have been done for."

No matter how much physical strength I had, if that strength couldn't reach then there was no meaning... As they say, there's power in numbers.

"I remember now!"

Leipin yelled suddenly, after mulling over Gordon's words.

"What's with you all of a sudden, old man Leipin?"

"Ryoma, could you show me your healing slime from earlier? I've only ever heard stories of healing slimes before."

"Sure."

I called the two healing slimes over and picked one up.

"Go ahead."

"Thank you. Hmm. Its body is white and rather minute for a slime species. I witnessed it using healing magic with my own eyes... It is exactly as I heard. Do you feed it the same as your other slimes?"

"Actually, it refuses to consume anything other than water. Cleaner slimes don't normally eat meat either, but they will when ordered to. I believe it's a matter of preference... but healing slimes only drink water. That would be the biggest difference."

"Oh my, is that true?"

"How does it live on just water?"

"It has a skill called photosynthesis. The skill takes in light and turns it into the nutrients needed for survival, so it's able to live off just water."

"There's such a skill as that?! Hmm, how fascinating… No, I believe there was a monster that had this skill in the plant-related monster encyclopedia…"

"Is that slime strong, nya?"

Miya asked, ignoring how Leipin was immersed in his own thoughts.

"It's extremely weak. It has no combat abilities at all and will lose to a normal slime."

"That is indeed weak, nya…"

"That's probably the reason why healing slimes are so rare. Even if a healing slime is born, it immediately gets killed by another monster or animal, leaving it no chance of being noticed by a human."

"Those without power cannot survive in the wild, after all… Healing slimes have no way of protecting themselves at all, yes?"

Ah, so Leipin was still listening.

"It's completely specialized towards enduring hits. On top of healing magic, it has a skill for life enhancement, so when attacked it will heal itself while fleeing."

"Enduring while fleeing, hmm."

"It's surprisingly hardy, but it wouldn't live for very long in the wild. They seem to know it too, as even when I tell them they can move freely they choose to stick to me or my other familiars. They're useful in how they'll heal me and the other slimes as soon as we're hurt, but I only keep them on healing duty. They're completely incapable of combat."

"I see... I've seen something good today. Thank you."

"It's rare to see someone show understanding for slime research. It was my pleasure."

"If there's anything you'd ever like to know about monsters, feel free to ask me. I'm confident I can answer most questions. And my conversations with you are always enlightening and interesting; it's strange why you didn't receive the correct evaluation."

Hearing that made Asagi join the conversation.

"I am not the most knowledgeable about tamers, but I have heard the more familiars thou hast the more difficult they are to control. Should not this many familiars be worthy in the eyes of the Tamer's Guild?"

"I'm newly registered with no achievements and the Tamer's Guild makes evaluations with emphasis on the strength of the familiar and rank, so different slime species cannot receive a high evaluation. If anything, there's a higher chance of attracting unwanted attention and elitism, so the guild didn't even announce my research results."

"Many people deem slimes to be incompetent and worthless. Ryoma discovered two new species in cleaner and scavenger slimes, both of which have extremely useful abilities. Personally, I think that and your research results are enough to raise your rank by several levels. However, as a monster researcher, once you know the social position of slimes you'll realize publicizing the knowledge that Ryoma currently has won't change their low reputation. It's understandable that Ryoma doesn't wish to publicize it. That's how deep-seated the worthless image of slimes is, both inside and outside of the Tamer's Guild..."

"Really? Even an uneducated person like me can tell how valuable those two species are. If I could use taming magic, I'd want them myself."

"If more people were as unprejudiced as you, perhaps the correct evaluation would be received one day."

Everyone nodded at Welanna's words. They all seemed to understand the worth of scavenger and cleaner slimes after the toilet cleaning incident and today.

Seeing them all gave me an idea.

"If I ran a laundromat, I could make enough money to live off…"

"Laundromat?"

I must have been thinking out loud.

"Just something that came to mind for me. If I used my cleaner slimes to offer adventurers laundry services that could clean even the worst goblin filth for cheap, would I be able to earn enough to survive?"

"How cheap is 'cheap?'"

"Let's see… What if I made exclusive bags and charged 1 small bronze coin each, at most 1 medium bronze?"

"THAT'S PERFECT!"

Everyone's voices answered at once.

"We all know first-hand how clean you can make them, nya. One bag for 1 medium bronze would be cheap."

"Especially today, with all that goblin blood and grease being so difficult to clean…"

"Thinking about the aftermath is always depressing, always…"

"I throw away my dirty clothes and buy new ones. The smell sticks through washes and I can't wear it again. There are many other beastkin like me with sharp senses of smell making decent money, and they would all pay 1 medium bronze for the filth and smell to be cleaned. It's cheaper than buying new, after all."

Beastkin were truly sensitive to scents, so the four beastkin ladies endorsed my idea eagerly.

"If it was that cost, non-adventurers would be interested too. Considering the labor and time needed for laundry, it'd be faster and easier to ask you to do it."

"I'd put in a request tomorrow if possible. The laundry at my house has piled up..."

"I'm terrible at housework in general. Especially when I get engrossed in my research, my laundry goes neglected. Every time that happens, I hire someone to take care of it, but it gets costly."

"In Leipin's case, the filth gets worse as it is left for so long, making the cost increase... But hiring help certainly costs a fair wage. Only wealthy families and nobles can afford such luxuries. In that regard, Ryoma's price sounds fair for commoners."

Were they all single or something? The four men added their rather sloppy perspectives, summarized by Asagi.

They were more interested than I expected, though...

"If you really go for it, I think it's more than plausible for you to make money. We'll be your customers too."

"But why were you considering such things?"

Ah, right, I hadn't told them why yet...

"Actually, I was thinking about some stuff yesterday. And I decided to become independent."

"What do you mean?"

"As you all know already, I came to this town together with the duke's family. And I've been in their care since... But recently, I realized I had been taking advantage of their kindness. So I discussed it with them and decided to cut off their support so I can be independent."

"You cut off the support from the duke's house?!"

"What a waste..."

"Though I cut their support off, I'm still staying in the accommodation provided by them... They've treated me incredibly well, and that gradually started to feel natural... I was being too spoiled. When they leave town, I'll refocus myself."

"Even so, who would normally do that? I can't imagine cutting off support from the duke. Though I'd never have the chance to do such a thing in the first place."

"Still, I like the way you think."

"Hahaha... And so, at the end of our discussion, I promised to take on a job for them and contact them regularly. Then I decided to stay in this town, so I was searching for ways to earn my own living costs. I intend on keeping at being an adventurer, but the job I took on from the duke requires my periodic return to this town. That's why I wanted to prepare several forms of income, so that I have a safety net if I am unable to continue being an adventurer."

"I see, that sounds great. Do your best."

"If you're staying in this town, then we'll be seeing you more in the future. I'll look forward to working with you again."

"Same here, I'll continue to be in your care."

Our trivial chatter continued until we returned to town on the last carriage.

When I returned to the inn, Eliaria and the others summoned me to their room.

"Welcome back!"

"Good work today, Ryoma."

"The job ended early today, didn't it? Is everything going well at the mines?"

"Huh? Have you not received contact yet?"

"We were at the public office today to inquire about the mines… It seems like they were left abandoned for a long time after all, did something happen?"

"We found a goblin village today, so we eliminated it. …There was even a goblin king, and it turned into quite the commotion."

Immediately after my report, voices of surprise shouted, "A goblin king?!"

"Was everything okay?!"

"Thankfully, I was given a role to stop fleeing goblins from escaping, so it wasn't a problem. Fortunately, there were no casualties either."

"I see, that's a relief…"

"But the nest was big enough to have a goblin king and goblin knights, and the number of goblins that fled to us was around 2000. Since it was that big of a job, we were dismissed after cleaning up the goblin corpses and told to rest."

"You all did well to have no casualties…"

"The goblin king was subjugated by high ranking adventurers, while us low ranked adventurers somehow pulled through using traps. And there's also one more thing."

I explained the circumstances I had heard from the six kids. That they were troubled after losing the toilet cleaning job.

Then, the ducal family looked a little disappointed.

"I see…"

"What's happening at the public office now? Whatever you're allowed to reveal is fine."

"We're dealing with and reorganizing the staff. The leaders of the crime are already behind bars, being investigated for further charges."

"What happened today will probably be presented as a result of what they did too. So the toilet cleaning is being taken care of by the guild?"

"That's right. I accepted a request once after that."

"The guild wouldn't want to keep their clients waiting, after all."

"I did tell the group that they could accept that job at the guild, and they'd be paid properly for it. They seemed doubtful, but motivated."

"Sorry… We'll talk to the new supervisor to do something about it."

The conversation stopped there.

"Now, let's set aside the gloomy talk. I'm glad you're safe."

"You must be hungry after such a big job. Do you want to eat something?"

"Yes please."

"Your slimes worked hard too, right? Do they need anything?"

"They've already eaten their fill of goblins today, enough to split tonight."

"Oh my, really? Which slimes will be increasing?"

"Acid, poison, cleaner, and some of the sticky slimes too."

"That will be quite the increase, then."

"They did eat a large amount. It's an increase in strength no matter which type increases, and they're useful for the production of waterproof materials and for improving the environment… but the amount of magic energy needed to make taming contracts is getting a bit too much."

"Since there are many of them, it can't be helped. Don't push yourself too hard."

"Yes. If I can't manage today, I'll split the contracts across two or three days."

"That would be good."

After that, we ate while chatting about my plans for the future, so I told them about how I was considering life as an adventurer while making money elsewhere at the same time.

Come to think of it, I hadn't asked how long they were all staying for... I should ask them that.

"How long will everyone be staying in town for? I haven't asked until now, but..."

"Didn't we tell you? Until the mass spawns of grell frogs stop. We'll remain in town for as long as we can, until Elia starts school."

Grell frogs were...

"The monster with the skin used for armor?"

"Yes, it is indeed used for armor. Its organs are also used in medicine. They spawn in the swamps around here in great numbers every year. We're taking Elia there."

"There's a red swamp in the forest, roughly halfway between town and the mines."

"Are you defeating the grell frogs?"

I wondered if it was training, but apparently not. They're training, but only as a bonus. Their real goal was the Limour Bird that flocked around the same time as the mass spawns.

"They're a very beautiful monster with blue wings. Their cries are also beautiful and they can fly very fast, making them a popular monster. However, they're difficult to capture and rarely any are ever tamed, so there isn't much chance to see them. But they gather around the swamp in flocks. You should take this chance to go see them too, Ryoma. They're worth the visit to see."

So not all monsters were to be feared... but if they ate grell frogs, that meant they were a carnivorous bird... The only carnivorous birds that came to mind were crows, which would pick at trash bags... But the colors made it like a peacock? ...I had no idea, but I was curious. I should go take a look if it's around, though.

"I'd love to see it as well."

"In that case, you can come along with us."

"Please take me with you when the mass spawns happen."

"Of course! We'll definitely go together!"

I made the promise with Eliaria and left their room after the meal.

Before sleeping, I let the slimes split and formed taming contracts, but my magic ran out halfway through so I left the rest for tomorrow. I still had some recovery potions, but it seemed like a waste to use them here.

❧ Chapter 2 Episode 19 ❧
Business Discussions (Part 1)

Monster Subjugation, Day 3.

Yesterday many people were injured in the goblin king fiasco, and the unruly adventurers were sacked the day before that. Thanks to that, the monster extermination progress was proceeding slower than planned.

After what happened yesterday, my party was disbanded. Jeff and the others were each given a group of low-ranked adventurers to instruct instead.

In my case, I didn't need to receive any instructions, but at the same time I was too inexperienced to be left in charge of others. And so, I was acting alone with my slimes.

It wouldn't affect my work at all. Cave bats and small rats were easily captured by making the sticky slimes spit their sticky solution onto their poles like birdlime and swing it around. Cave mantises were taken care of quickly by lance-wielding poison slimes that could jab between their blades from outside of their reach, and were then eaten on the spot.

For some reason, these slimes were gaining their own individual strength on top of their usual power in numbers until now... And for some reason, watching them fight cave mantises reminded me of watching that thing... What was it, that game that was on Earth? It really boomed for a while. The theme song was so light and carefree, yet I remember for some reason the lyrics were rather bloodthirsty.

I worked at the monster extermination with enough leeway to be thinking about such things.

And so, the morning ended without any particular incident. Well, things like yesterday shouldn't happen every day.

I did spot a group of five goblins, but they didn't have any reinforcements, and when I reported it, it was determined that they were survivors from yesterday, putting an end to that case.

For the afternoon shift, I started experimenting with sticky slime fighting styles.

For example, having them proceed down the mineshaft by sticking to the ceiling and hanging their bodies down. The way cave bats flew around everywhere was just so annoying, they reminded me of flies — and so I had the slimes imitate flypaper. As a result, they stuck easily and were quickly consumed.

Furthermore, when I ordered the most nimble sticky slime to immediately turn its body into a net after jumping, it was able to do it. When I grabbed that slime and threw it, it opened into a net midair and caught many cave bats on its way down to the ground.

Using another sticky slime, I did the same thing.

…And again.

…And again.

…An average of four to five cave bats were caught each time.

This seemed like it would be useful for many things too! Sticky slimes were sure useful! It seemed like sticky slimes had a wide range of uses. They were a slime useful in both battle and daily life.

Excited with this discovery, I continued using the sticky slimes to gather together the small monsters until the work day was over.

Then, that evening.

As I was returning to town via carriage after work, the carriage wheel broke down just as we reached the town. Although no one was particularly hurt, the carriage had rocked suddenly and sharply. Since it would be dangerous to continue like that, the other passengers and I alighted to finish the journey on foot.

"Well, a walk would be nice too."

The sun had set over the town, and the scent of dinner wafted in the air. It must have been the restaurants in the area. Eager people were already drinking at this time, as I could occasionally hear cheerful voices. As I was enjoying the peaceful atmosphere on my walk, I passed before Serge's Morgan Trading Company.

…Come to think of it, the magic recovery potions I received from him really saved us yesterday… I might be able to see some bags to use as reference for my laundry service too. Guess I could drop by for a bit.

When I wandered into the store casually, Serge was talking to a female store attendant at the counter.

"Welcome, Master Ryoma!"

He spotted me with his sharp eyes and immediately invited me through to the office. Even though I was happy to wait if he was in the middle of work…

"What are you here for today?"

"The magic recovery potions I received from you the other day were a great help in a job I had yesterday, so I wanted to thank you, for one. There's also something I want, so I was wondering if you knew of any other good stores."

"I see, I'm glad to hear the products of our stores were useful to you. It's an honor to have you visit my store in search of something. What did you need?"

"I'm looking for a fair number of sturdy bags, it doesn't matter if the material is cheap. As for the size… I haven't decided yet."

"Oh? May I ask what they will be used for?"

"It's a bit of a long story, but actually…"

Here, I explained my decision to pursue my own independence to Serge's surprise but admiration, before he showed interest in my idea to run a laundry service.

"A side job between adventurer work, considering options once you've retired from adventurer work… You are very well prepared for someone of your age, Master Ryoma."

That's because I was actually 42… I'm not sure what I was like compared to other older men in Japan, but I was at least prepared enough to know I was doing a dangerous job. I'd never heard of insurance or pensions in this world either. Even if they existed, the conditions to get them would be very strict.

"No, no, I'm not that impressive."

"You're too modest… But a laundry service, hmm? One bag for 1 small bronze to 1 medium bronze does seem like a fair price that would be used by both adventurers and commoners. However, you'd also have to hire personnel to do the laundry, and you need to produce results that satisfy the customers. Even if you can manage it alone to start, if your clients increase you may find yourself unable to keep up."

Ah, I forgot to tell him about cleaner slimes.

"There's one thing I forgot to mention. Please wait a moment."

I brought out one cleaner slime from my dimension home.

"This is my familiar, a type of slime called a cleaner slime."

"Oh? I've never heard of such a slime."

"This is a new species of slime I discovered by coincidence. I submitted the information to the Tamer's Guild, but at present I am the only one in this world that possesses a contract with one."

The gods themselves had told me it was a new species, so there shouldn't be tamed cleaner slimes other than mine.

"What does that slime have to do with things?"

"This slime possesses a skill called cleanse, which allows it to eat only dirt and filth. Naturally, the items it eats the filth off of are then cleaned. More so than if they had been washed normally."

At my words, Serge's mouth fell open wordlessly. I guess it was hard to believe after all…

I decided to give him a live demonstration instead.

"It may be hard to imagine with just words. Have a look at this instead. This cloth is a goblin's loincloth, obtained from the job today. If you'd like, I can show you how the slime eats the filth and turns it into a clean cloth right before your eyes."

Serge gulped at my words and nodded, answering curtly, "Yes, please do."

"Would you like to appraise it just in case?"

"Yes, I shall. Though with this wretched scent, there's no mistaking that it's a goblin's loincloth…"

Serge said with a light laugh, appraising it. After he confirmed from the appraisal result that it was indeed a cloth from a goblin, I handed it to the cleaner slime. The cleaner slime took the fabric into its body like usual, then churned it around like a washing machine. The cloth became cleaner and cleaner right before our eyes, until finally the cleaner slime spat the cloth out onto the table in the office. It took less than 30 seconds in total for all of this.

Serge hesitantly picked up the cloth that was clearly a different color to earlier and appraised it. The appraisal result must have come up with a clean cloth, as he grabbed my hand in excitement and started praising me for cleaning a goblin's filthy loincloth into such pristine fabric.

My hands were still dirty from touching the goblin's loincloth earlier… Serge seemed to realize that from the look on my face, and frowned slightly. It was the perfect time to explain what it was like to take a cleaner slime bath and let him experience it. On the hands only, of course.

Afterward, he appraised his own hands carefully, then returned to giving me the flurry of praise.

This person… I could tell Serge was a good person, he never looked down upon me for my appearance. But being on the receiving end of all his compliments was tiring too…

"I apologize for acting so shamefully before you. But this slime is truly wonderful! With this slime, I'm sure Master Ryoma's laundry business can open with no issue. Price, speed, and result… I can see your business flourishing before my eyes."

He seemed to be tripping…

"Anyway, I was wondering what size bag would be good for this? Embarrassing as it is to admit, I have no knowledge of the market regarding this."

"Let's see… Let me arrange for several to be brought here," Serge said, ordering one of his servants to bring several bags here.

"As you can see, they increase in size from left to right. The furthest on the left would hold enough for one set of adult clothing."

"I think a slightly bigger one would be better. Families would have more clothes than that, and single men tend to find laundry so bothersome they let it accumulate. Also, I think customers would find it more worth their money if they could have four or five outfits washed with one medium bronze coin, rather than one outfit per coin. The amount of labor on my side doesn't change that much whether it's one outfit or five, so as long as I can earn the minimum amount I need to live I won't seek much compensation in exchange. I think it would be more profitable to have a cheap fee so that many people repeatedly use the service."

Small profits with quick returns is what I relied on in my previous life too... For example, the beef place I went to for lunch.

The stores I used to visit were practically all set in stone. From the viewpoint of the stores back then, I must have been a repeat customer. I don't know how much I paid in total to the stores in my past life's neighborhood, but I never had complaints. I was grateful that they supported my past lifestyle.

Based on that thought, securing repeat customers was an important thing, and a cheap fee would be a powerful weapon in doing so. Of course, that's assuming that the work done was satisfactory.

As I was thinking such things, for some reason, Serge started watching me with a glint in his eye...

"Wonderful. Master Ryoma has a wonderful mind for management, looking into the future instead of being blinded by the profits under his nose. I, Serge Morgan, am most impressed."

What was this strange feeling? I was only speaking from experience in my past life, but the amount of praise I was receiving had surpassed the realms of discomfort and gone straight into guilt-inducing territory... I felt sorry for the people in Japan seriously studying business administration... Well, I suppose if I thought of it as brainstorming...

"In that case, what do you think of these bags? A bag of this size could fit two days' worth of clothes for an average three- to four-person family."

"Yes, it also seems good as it could also hold a week's worth for one person. I shall go with that. Could you prepare two to three bags twice that size, as well as five times that size?"

"It can be arranged, but wouldn't that be too large?"

"If the earlier bag is to be used on an individual level, the twice as big bag would be used for small groups, such as adventurer parties. The five times as big bag could be used for large groups, such as blacksmiths with many apprentices, or workers at construction sites."

For example…

"At a rate of one outfit per day, the individual bag can hold seven outfits' worth. Twice that would be 14 outfits, and five times that would be able to hold 35 outfits. If the individual bag is 1 medium bronze, it'd be 10 sutes. The double-sized bag can be 1 medium bronze and 8 small bronze coins, at 18 sutes. Then the five-times large bag can be 4 medium bronzes, or 40 sutes for a group discount. What do you think of this? More people would consider the service if it had a discount, and if there aren't enough people to fill a group bag, then they might gather others, spreading news of the laundry service… Also, more people would mean dirty laundry would also build up faster. One person would take 14 days to fill a bag, but 14 people would take one day… The more customers I have, the more money I can collect daily, and the customers would pay less per person. Looking at it from a long-term perspective, it would definitely bring a profit, so I think I should push for that to gain business."

Brainstorming — the act of suggesting ideas without evaluating the contents. It had been a while, but I was still surprisingly capable.

"Blacksmiths and construction sites are particularly dirty workplaces, so their clothes would definitely need cleaning. In those cases, the workers who come to learn about the laundry service through their jobs might bring their personal clothes on an individual basis too. They're also mostly filled with men, so there should be quite a few people who hate cleaning, or find it bothersome. In fact, when I asked some adventurers today… If they spread word of it at their jobs, then those types of clientele too could…"

It was at this point that I noticed Serge's state.

...Ah. Ah! I messed up... Serge was frozen with rounded eyes... I've always had the bad habit of talking too much one-sidedly... Who knew how many times I failed at creating social and work relationships in my previous life because of this... Was my focus slipping because I hadn't talked about work-like things in such a long time?

⇌ Chapter 2 Episode 20 ⇌
Business Discussions (Part 2)

At any rate, I had to do something about Serge…

"Sorry, I have a bad habit of rattling on and on by myself sometimes… If I've made you feel uncomfortable, I apologize."

"Oh, no no no! Not at all, not at all! I'm just a little surprised. Master Ryoma is only 11 years old, yet you keep coming up with such effective-sounding ideas."

Really?! …Come to think of it, I was an 11-year-old child. Even if it was something simple, I suppose anyone would be surprised to see a child thinking about business strategies… There were parents that would wildly rejoice just to see their baby stand up. Normally no one would ask a baby to do the same things as an adult. Perhaps that was why I was seen so highly?

And they were less my ideas and more my interpretations of modern advertisement strategies… They were simple calculations full of flaws. Rather, didn't they have discounts here?

"Umm, do people not do discounts normally?"

"There are discounts, but I haven't heard of their use as a permanent tactic… Most are applied when merchants want to seem better to their customer, or when they want to make a quick sale. Discounting recklessly would only increase losses. Otherwise, they're sometimes used to make annoying customers leave faster… Or in some nastier stores, some merchants will set the product to an outrageous price and discount it to make it seem like a steal."

He seemed to be saying that seriously...

"In this case, I would recommend that Master Ryoma registers at the Merchant's Guild."

"The Merchant's Guild?"

"Yes. There's a branch in this town as well, so you can register right away. Each kingdom has their own Merchant's Guild that manages all the trade of the kingdom, from peddlers to stalls and carts. You must go through the guild to start a business."

Eh?! Then...

"Then, was I about to do something illegal?"

"No no, the guild manages the trade of the kingdom, but that doesn't mean it oversees everything. Remote villages can sell things to each other of their own accord, and you're also permitted to sell medicinal herbs you gather to an apothecary. There's no issue in children or adventurers doing jobs for compensation without going through the guild either. As long as it isn't an extravagantly high price, it isn't considered illegal, and there's no problem as long as both parties agree. However, based on what you have said today, there is plenty of possibility you'll be making quite an income. You may attract the guild's attention for finding a new source of money."

"That was close... Thank you, Mr. Serge."

"Not at all, it seems like I had underestimated you, Master Ryoma. I never imagined you would have such a mind for business. I omitted information about registration, believing you were just making pocket change between your time doing adventurer work."

No, it was exactly as you presumed. I hadn't thought very far earlier... But for now I'd take him up on it.

"In that case, if I were to run a laundry service I should register with the guild. I'm already registered with the Adventurer's Guild and Tamer's Guild, would that be a problem?"

"Rest assured, I will put forth a recommendation for you when you register, so you won't face any issues. Having people across different guilds brings in more information, so it's actually welcomed. How would you like to go register tomorrow? I shall accompany you."

"Tomorrow... I still have adventurer work, so I'll only be back around the same time as today."

"That is fine. There are always several employees staffed in the Merchant's Guild, so registration can be completed at any time. For merchants, information is our livelihood. We need to be able to deliver information while it's still fresh."

A 24-hour business...?

"In that case, if it's all right with you."

"Why, of course!"

Whoa?!

"The laundry service you've formulated is a wonderful idea! It has the potential to bring in a large profit, no other merchants are yet to set their eyes on it, and it could create a stir among the business in this world! I, Serge Morgan, will gladly lend you what little power I have!"

He started giving some grand monologue?! I didn't expect such a fuss... I was only hoping for a little extra pocket money...

"Th-Thank you very much. That's most reassuring."

"Your words are wasted on me. Now that it's come to this, we must think about where to open your store."

Store?! I hadn't planned on doing anything at such a large scale, though!

"Hmm... That look on your face tells me you weren't planning on doing anything so grand, am I correct?"

"Yes. I was only thinking of earning the minimum amount of money to survive, at most. That's why a stall on a street corner would have been fine, or I could have gone around to each household myself. If I had a storefront, I wouldn't be able to work as an adventurer."

"I see. However, if it's management of a store, you needn't worry. I can lend you some of my store staff."

No, that wouldn't work.

"Even if I had a store, leaving it to other people is a bit…"

When I said that, Serge gave a bitter laugh and said, "Hmm… I think I'm starting to understand what the duke's people were saying… Master Ryoma, there's nothing untoward about leaving the management to others, you know?"

Huh?

"While it's true that most people start their own stores by doing the management themselves, when you reach my level you may have many branches. In which case, it would be impossible for me to oversee all of the stores by myself. Ergo, I select subordinates I can trust, train them, and leave them in charge instead. What would be so strange about that?"

When he put it that way, he had a point… It was common in Japan for chain stores to have hired store managers that weren't the owners either…

"True, there's nothing strange about that."

"That's right. Furthermore, there are people in this world who are more suited for management, and people who are less suited. Rather than having someone unsuited force themselves to do it, it would be better for the store to simply hire someone suitable instead."

"That I understand, too."

"As for you, Master Ryoma… At this point in time, I cannot make a judgment yet. Your ideas and practical business mind makes you suitable for management in a way, but I don't see you being able to size up your competitors. Your thoughts can be clearly read from your face."

Was I really that obvious?!

"Considering your age, I'm sure you're able to hide more than someone else that young would, but it wouldn't work on any veteran merchant."

"I see…"

I was fairly confident in my poker face in my past life too… Was it all just my imagination?

"Also, I am not lending you my personnel entirely out of my own goodwill either. Lord Reinhart ordered me to help you out if you ever came to me, and I also believe in the promise I see in you."

"Promise… you see…?"

"Yes. Even without Lord Reinhart's recommendation, I would have had my eye on you for inventing waterproof fabric and thread, as well as creating all those ingots at such a young age. On top of that, I can also expect today's discussion to lead to great profits in the future. There is no way I could ignore this as a merchant. I want to be involved in any way possible, even if it were through paying for a bag of my own at your store. If you need opening funds, I'm also willing to invest in it."

…If he's willing to go that far, then I guess…? But still…

"What if you invest into the store and it fails?"

"It would be impossible to open a store while fearing failure. Even merchants with relatively large stores are burdened by some kind of risk or another. More than anything, I believe there is a high likelihood that your store will bring profits. Even in the case that it fails, you can simply repay the loss to me by making iron ingots and waterproof fabric and thread. Operation fees should be quite low if you're leaving the cleaning to your slimes, so the damages won't be as great. There's a high chance of success, and there's even a way to make up for failure. I can't imagine any of the usual traps would apply here, so no real merchant would pass up this chance."

I see. I certainly could make money if I made iron ingots…

"I understand. I shall lean on you for your assistance."

"Do you now see things from my point of view?"

"Yes. However, I'll hold back from accepting any financial investments for the time being. Fortunately, I have some funds from bandit bounties I earned in the past."

"Then just the personnel?"

"Please. Also, if you could let me buy any miscellaneous items needed for a store at your shop, starting with the bags. I will bring ingots in when I have time, separate from this discussion. I was planning on making them in the first place, since I was left in charge of the mines."

"Thank you. I hope good business comes to both of us in the future."

Thus, with the conversation wrapped up, I purchased the bags from Serge and left the store.

■　■　■

After walking along the dark path back, I was met by a fuming Eliaria waiting at the inn.

"My lady…?"

"Ryoma, what were you doing out so late? I was worried…"

Eliaria'a fuming aura settled, and then she started crying. It seemed like after everything with the goblin king yesterday, she had been really worried.

My bad.

Accepting my fault, I silently listened to her scold me through her tears. Eventually, she was worn out by her own crying and anger and said she was going to bed, leaving me to watch her walk away with the maids.

"I'm very sorry for worrying you."

"It's all right now; it seems Elia has scolded you enough for it."

"It's true that we were worried, though."

"Take more care next time."

"Yes, I shall bear that in mind."

"And? What were you doing out this late?"

I explained how the carriage broke down and I dropped by Serge's shop when I was walking past.

"So you were at Serge's, huh? And I see you're already thinking about your new job."

"I'll probably be back late again tomorrow. I'm sorry, I know I was just scolded today…"

"As long as you let us know in advance, it's fine. What are you doing tomorrow?"

"I'm going to register at the Merchant's Guild with Mr. Serge. While we were discussing things, the scale grew larger and larger until it required registration at the guild."

"What? Wasn't it just an odd job to add to your living income?"

"That's what I intended on at first, but I was talked into opening a store by Mr. Serge."

"A store? Your discussion must have progressed quite a bit."

"Mr. Serge said he could see a 'prosperous future in store.' The store attendants will also be provided by his shop."

"To think Serge would say such high praise… So when will you open?"

He just asked about the opening date without batting an eye?! I expected more shock.

"There are still many things to decide about the store… But how come none of you are surprised that an 11-year-old child is saying they'll open a store?"

"It's not like there's an age restriction to these things, after all. Children your age have stalls all the time, and many of them act as store attendants too."

"While there aren't any that can open their own store at 11, we are talking about you here."

"You aren't a regular child, after all. If Serge has given his stamp of approval, then it should be fine. But if anything happens, make sure you lean on us, okay? Don't forget to contact us regularly."

Was that really okay?

"I understand."

After that, I returned to my room in a daze and finished letting the leftover slimes from yesterday split, forming contracts with them.

The updated slime count went like this:

Sticky Slime x907
Poison Slime x666
Acid Slime x666
Cleaner Slime x22
Scavenger Slime x3033
Healing Slime x2
Metal Slime x1
Slime x1

The number of sticky slimes had exceeded 900, nearly reaching 1000.

The poison slimes and acid slimes had reached the same number. But 666 was a little unlucky...

I was happy to see the cleaner slimes double in number. And the slimes seemed to be stronger, perhaps because of the goblin fight yesterday? Their physical attack resistance in big- and huge-slime form was good. But I had never imagined slimes could learn staff mastery and spear mastery or unarmed combat...

I'd thought of many things to teach them, but I didn't expect the slimes to pick up these skills. I should try to teach them more things in the future...

⇜ Chapter 2 Episode 21 ⇝
Instant Decision

Monster Subjugation, Day 4.

After finishing work at the mines, I returned to town and headed for Serge's place.

"Good evening, Mr. Serge."

"I've been waiting for you, Master Ryoma. Shall we get going?"

The carriage that was prepared took us from the center of town to a little towards the south.

We eventually reached the Merchant's Guild, a plain building that was simple but sturdy, faint light shining out of the front door. Though sparse, I could hear the sound of people other than employees within, too.

When we walked up to the reception, they let us straight through to a room further inside. In response to the experienced manner he conveyed his business, the receptionist lady bowed her head politely. Seeing that exchange made me wonder if Serge was treated as a fairly important figure.

He was the president of a large trading company, so I guess so?

Several minutes later, a scrawny man and an old, hunchbacked lady entered the room. The two of us both made to stand up when the old lady stopped us with a hand and the man opened his mouth.

"What's this, Serge? Been a helluva time since I last saw ya's. Ain't heard yer name on the grapevine lately, jes' been wonderin' what'cher up ta nowadays."

He said in a… fake-sounding accent? There was a nostalgic lilt to his words that made me wonder how it was being translated in my ears. I used to have a boss who sounded like this…

"Long time no see, Pioro."

"What are you here for today? It's rare to see you around these parts outside of guild gatherings. I haven't met that boy there before, have I? I'm Glissela. The hag in charge of this Merchant's Guild."

"I'm Ryoma Takebayashi. I've come to register for the Merchant's Guild today. Though I am still inexperienced, I humbly ask for your guidance and instruction."

"Oh my, what a polite greeting. Serge, is this boy one of your servants?"

"Bingo. Howdy, name's Pioro Saionji. If y'need anything from me, I'm happy t'indulge ya."

"Nice to meet you. I'm Ryoma Takebayashi."

Saionji? That was a very Japanese-sounding last name. His black hair and eyes almost made his appearance look Japanese… Was he a descendant of an otherworlder?

"Ryoma. Roight, I'll commit that t' me mem'ry. So, like the ol' crone Gli said, what brings ya 'round here, Serge?"

"We're just here for Ryoma's guild registration. I'm simply an escort."

At Serge's words, the other two looked at me. Then, the guildmaster peered closely at my face.

"Hmm… Wait a minute."

After saying that, she picked up her staff and bopped Serge on the head with it.

"You fool! What are you doing, making a child act in consideration of you!" she scolded.

"Ow, guildmaster, not the staff…"

"I don't know what the situation is, but he seems like an earnest child. Being revered by a decades-older man like you will only make him feel awkward and uncomfortable."

How did she know what I was secretly thinking?! Could she read minds?!

"Ryoma, was it? I can't read minds."

She clearly could!

"I may be old, but my merchant senses are still sharp as a tack. You seem like the honest type, so I can read you a fair bit."

"I see…"

"Terrifying ol' bint, ain't she? She always tells people that, but I jes' about figger she *can* read minds."

"Rather than terrifying, I think it's amazing. But I've always been bad at reading other people's thoughts."

"It's all experience. If you place yourself in the right environment, you'll gradually learn with time. You're only just starting out. It seems like things have happened in your past… but your future starts now."

"Thank you… Are you sure you can't read minds?"

"Don't be ridiculous. I could tell because of the distant look in your eyes when you mentioned other people's thoughts."

Seriously?!

"Did I really have such a look in my eyes?"

"It reminded me of a middle-aged man looking back on his past."

She's right!

"Now, set your shock aside. You came for guild registration, yes? The night's getting late, so let's get it done with."

She handed me the registration form.

For some reason, she had one on hand… Could she really… Oh well, guess I'll fill it out first.

"Hmm… What does it mean by occupation type? Isn't a merchant an occupation?"

"You write the business you want to do there. So if you want to sell weapons, you write in 'weapons merchant.' You can write more than one, and you can always add more later, so you don't have to write any you're unsure of right now. Basic types of occupations are listed on the back, so you can reference those."

"I understand."

Come to think of it, I'd heard of adventurers working as peddlers before… For now, I'll add that… And for my main store, a town merchant? I wrote that down too.

…What was this bard occupation? I knew what the word meant, but was this a merchant too?

As I thought such things, I finished filling in the registration form and submitted it to the guildmaster, who looked at it and said, "Oh, you're an adventurer? Take care of yourself out there; there's no coming back from death. And you want your own store?"

"Actually, I had a bit of a different idea for a store. I was thinking of doing it as a side job between my adventurer work at first, but Mr. Serge told me to register at the guild and do it at a larger scale."

"Serge did?"

"Oh? How curious. What kinda business?"

"A laundry service."

"Laundry service? You're going to take money for washing? … Serge, why would he need registration for that? There's nothing to lose by registering, but it's not something to go out of your way to do."

"I thought the same at first. But after listening to Master Ryoma, I realized he had the potential to make enough profits to be a problem if he didn't register."

"…He got that much potential, y'say?"

"I'd like to hear the details myself, if it's that good of an idea."

Serge sent me a smiling look. It should be safe to tell these two, but I'll leave it to Serge in case I say anything wrong. As the explanation continued, their reactions gradually changed from surprise to understanding, eventually turning into laughter.

"Heehee! Living a long life sure brings about some interesting sights! Ryoma, you've come up with something great here. Who would have imagined a slime could have such use? And a new species of slime, at that. This is a good omen for sure."

"Damn straight. If ya could pull that off, ya'd be makin' 'er rain. The guild would really start t'stir shit up if ya didn't register. For such a ripe young lad as yerself, ya sure got some interestin' plans fer business. Gods bless ya."

For some reason, Pioro started praying in my direction. What was this person doing?

"You don't have to pay Pioro any attention. He's always doing that when he meets someone with a good plan for profits."

"Luck's somethin' only the gods can give ya. I see someone 'bout ta stir up some mad bank, I gotta show my gratitude, d'ya not agree?"

I guess I could understand.

"I figger I've got enough feelin's of surprise fer th'next 8 years. But yeah, that sorta business'd be a long shot fer me. Puttin' the idea aside, a laundry service ain't gonna make no profits without that slime. Only you could git 'er done. So buck up, lad, I'm sure yer gonna do fine."

"I've taken a liking to you. Nothing usually shakes me anymore in my old age, but… You have promise, so come visit me every now and then. I'll serve tea and snacks, and listen to anything you have to say."

"Thank you. I'll do my best."

"Then next, let's decide your store location. Guildmaster, if you would, please."

"Good grief, Serge, treat your elders more kindly. Pioro, bring me the documents on the left bookcase. Top shelf, second from the right."

"Treat kindly, me foot! Cain't ya go get it yerself?!"

"Just go and get it."

"All right, all right... What, ain't this the document with all them defective buildings? Ryoma's store's got big potential, couldn't ya put 'im somewhere slightly better? I'd be willin' ta throw some funds in if he needs 'em too."

"You fool, Serge has already said the boy is oddly earnest. Even if you offer him money, he'd just turn it down."

I've been completely read through in such a short time, huh. I have been called overly serious and foolishly honest in the past, though. And I don't want to start a store with other people's money. Debts shouldn't be made lightly, and I had no intention of going that far to start my store.

The observation senses of a merchant were scary... There was something to fear in soft power.

"Now, as Pioro said, this stack of documents is a collection of buildings that are defective in some way. But that makes them that much cheaper, and very strictly speaking, you only need a place for a reception and storage, right?"

"Yes. The work will all be done by slimes, so I don't need a water source either."

"Normally if you heard someone was doing a laundry service with no need for water you'd wonder if they were just messing about, but... How much coin have you got prepared?"

"I have 700 small gold coins."

"That's more than expected."

"There were bandits near my old residence, and I defeated them with poison. Apparently, they had high bounties on their heads."

"If you have that much, then… Guildmaster. There was an empty lot near my store; how about that?"

"Let's see… there certainly was one…"

The guildmaster shuffled through the documents.

"Ah, here it is. It's in a spot facing the residential area. There was a large pub and inn, and a warehouse for storage, so the location's good. However, the inn caught on fire and over half the building turned to ash. It's overgrown and unusable right now. If you want to use it, you'd have to demolish the previous building and prepare the land for rebuilding. It's leftover land no one wants to buy because of the time and money investment involved. There are no flaws other than the building and land preparation, but what do you think?"

"I've heard that you are a very skilled earth magician. This spot is large and will allow you to build as you please."

There was a certain charm to being able to build how I liked.

"If you can use earth magic, would you be able to fix something up with time?"

"Let me think…"

If I used earth magic like Create Block, then used the hardening solution of my sticky slimes… Yeah, it could work.

"I can. Looking at this map, it really is a good location, so close to the residential area."

Gimul was a town that was surrounded by a sturdy wall elliptically long from north to south.

A large road cut straight through the center of the town, connecting the north gate to the south gate. The east was the residential area, while the west was the industrial area for ironworks and things.

There were many inns near the south gate, and the inn I was staying at was at the south too.

Because the north gate led to the mines (the abandoned mine), it wasn't really used by anyone other than mine workers. I had heard it hadn't been used much since the mines were abandoned.

There was a road to more mines from the east gate too, and these mines weren't abandoned. The residential area had been prepared in the east to make it easier for the miners to travel to work.

The building I had been introduced to just now was pretty much directly east of the center of town, right between the residential area and the main street. It was close to both the residential area and the Adventurer's Guild, and while the industrial area to the west was slightly further, the path there was simple. It really was the best possible location.

When I voiced my thoughts out loud, the guildmaster agreed.

"That's right. That's why this used to be a popular pub too. Lots of people used to gather there, like adventurers and residents on their way home. Even now, it'll attract people if you open it up there, but you'll need the funds to do so."

"I see... then I'll take that one."

Honestly, I didn't know much about location, but I couldn't imagine this was a bad one. It had the benefit of being close to the residential area and the Adventurer's Guild, and the appeal of building it how I wished. I was here at Serge's recommendation, and the guildmaster and Pioro seemed like nice people. I should be able to trust them.

"Are you sure?"

"Yes. I have no complaints about the location, and I should be able to do something about the demolishing, preparation, and reconstruction of the building with my magic and slime familiars. More than anything, I'm interested in the idea of building my own store from scratch."

"Like I said before, this place will be fairly expensive. It costs 580 small gold coins. And because the area is so large, the land tax will cost 10 small golds, and 60 small golds for the business license and yearly fees. It'll be a total of 650, are you sure?"

"That's no problem. I have some leeway in my living expenses."

"True, you'd be able to live like a noble or better for the rest of the year on 50 small golds alone... All right, this land is now yours, Ryoma. Also, I forgot to mention earlier, but the business license is only charged once at registration, while the land tax is doubled when buying. From next year onwards you'll only need to pay 5 small golds in annual land tax. Make sure you get it right."

"I understand. Thank you very much."

They told me several things after that, but it didn't seem like being a store owner in this world was that hard. All you have to do is buy land or a building from the guild and open a business there. The account book just needed to keep a record of income and expenses, and a tax based on the profits had to be paid to the guild along with the annual land tax. As long as you did that, neither age nor gender mattered.

The problem came down to whether I could earn anything and pay the money, I guess...

Furthermore, it seemed like the double land tax I paid this time was comparable to a deposit and gratuity fee on Earth. The business license varied depending on the scale of the business, so a stall could pay 5 medium bronze coins while the size of land I purchased cost me 2 small golds.

Finally, the yearly fees were kind of like a donation to the guild. Normally the yearly fee was a small sum, but there was no upper limit and the more you paid the more you were expressing your financial ability to do so, leading to preferential treatment from the guild and a higher evaluation. How business-like.

Once I had finished all the procedures, I thanked the three of them and left the guild.

Serge was due to appear at a guild gathering in the near future, which he had things to discuss with the guildmaster and Pioro about, so I said goodbye to him at the guild.

It looks like I'd be working on construction after my current job at the guild was done... I hadn't built a non-cavern residence since my previous life. Work was hard back then, but I also found it fun seeing the results happening right before my eyes.

I was kind of looking forward to it.

⇌ Chapter 2 Episode 22 ⇌
Store Setup 1

Monster Subjugation, Day 5 & Store Construction, Day 1.

"Ryoma, a little help, nya…"

During lunch break at the mines, Miya came over after I had received my meal and was resting. Behind her were Jeff, Asagi, Leipin and the others, and they were all covered in blood. I wonder what happened…

"Could you get rid of this blood for me? It smells so bad, I can't stand it."

"Is that goblin blood? Someone definitely went all-out again."

I swiftly gave my cleaner slime the order to clean the seven of them.

"Ah, I'm finally clean… Ryoma's cleaner slimes sure are useful."

"A relief it is. It would have been quite a horrendous ordeal to fetch lunch in my previous state."

"Honestly, Jeff's work is so sloppy."

"I already apologized…"

After the seven of them grabbed their lunches, we ate together and chatted. Apparently, they had eliminated a newly discovered goblin nest. They were survivors from last time, but the size of the nest was small enough for the seven of them and several others to deal with. The problem was after the subjugation. While they were cleaning up the corpses, Jeff had gone for the extravagant method of stabbing bodies with his spear, catching them on the tip and flinging them all to one spot.

208

"Though it accelerated the clean-up efforts, the resulting pile was unstable. It collapsed as we were on the brink of returning."

While they could evade the falling corpses, there was no evading the blood spray from them — Leipin even got hit directly by a falling body.

"It was a mess…"

"Damn right. If it weren't for Ryoma, we'd have to eat our lunch and work the afternoon shift in that smelly state."

"It really is amazing how you can remove goblin filth so easily."

"Thank you very much."

That was when I remembered I had yet to tell the seven of them about my laundry business.

"Speaking of which, do you recall how I mentioned doing a possible laundry service?"

"I do. What about it?"

"I'm going to be going ahead with that."

"Oh, really? From when?"

"The store isn't ready yet, so it'll be some time in the future. The price will be as I mentioned the other day, 1 medium bronze coin."

"Store? You're going to have a shopfront?"

"I discussed it with a merchant acquaintance and decided on that. I've already registered with the Merchant's Guild, and I was able to purchase land with some old bandit bounties. I'll either hire employees from the guild or work with the merchant for some help, so I can continue as an adventurer too."

"I see. It's a surprise to see someone so young owning a store, but that should have been a given. I, and all the adventurers who know of your slimes' abilities, of course, will definitely be using your service. Such an odd business will also spread like wildfire on the grapevine. If it flourishes, you may have trouble running it alone."

"While it wouldn't be impossible, he would lose time to work as an adventurer."

"Indeed. The scale of my idea turned out larger than I expected, but I can continue to work as an adventurer, so it'll work out. I'll inform you of the opening date, so please come use the service. There's also a discount offer for people who come in large groups."

"Oh, really? Then I should invite someone along…"

"Ryoma's already like a merchant, nya."

"He had a polite manner of speaking to begin with, so it doesn't feel out of place at all."

We finished our meals while discussing things, then worked diligently into the afternoon.

■　■　■

"This here is your land, Master Ryoma."

"It really is big."

After work, I visited Serge's place to check on the land I had purchased.

Before me was a two-story building standing on the verge of collapse, located on a plot of land slightly smaller than a kiddy baseball field. Roughly 20 meters by 40 meters, perhaps? Area-wise, it was probably larger than Serge's store.

It looked smaller on the map, though…

"The pub that used to be here was also an inn, after all. There were guest rooms and a warehouse."

"I see… and I can really do as I please with this?"

"Yes. As long as it's within the land, you may act freely. Will you be starting work today?"

"Let's see. I think I'll weed the place and start on the demolition today."

I took the scavenger slimes out of my Dimension Home and ordered them to eat the grass away from the building. That should take care of the weeding.

I kept an eye on the gradually dwindling overgrown grass as I put up a soundproof barrier around the building and demolished it bit-by-bit from the roof down. With all my caution for noise and safety, the neighbors shouldn't be affected.

Once I destroyed the entire ceiling, I changed the side walls to dirt with Break Rock. After checking the ceiling rubble, ruined furniture, and the dirt of walls to make sure they were safe, I shoved them all outside and cleaned up the inside.

I dismantled the remaining framework and posts with Windcutter.

All my limited construction knowledge came from the simple tasks I did at my part-time job... Or so it should have been, but I was bestowed with knowledge for my skill level when I came to this world so I could plan a simple building if I tried now. I also knew how to demolish something so that a building would fall in the right spots, making this extremely easy.

The architecture skill was amazing. Magic was so convenient.

In roughly one hour, half the weeds in the plot had been removed and half the building demolished, but it was getting late so I decided to head back.

For the record, Serge had been watching the entire time I was working, shocked at my number of slimes and tremendous amount of magic energy as I brute-forced my way through the tasks.

■ ■ ■

Monster Subjugation, Day 6 & Store Construction, Day 2.

Today was the last day of the monster subjugation at the mines. So many things had happened along the way, but the guildmaster informed us all that the mission was complete with this.

However, I was to be managing this place in the future. Even if I got busy, I had to do it properly. At the very least, I should patrol once a week until I lived elsewhere. As I was thinking that, the guildmaster summoned me.

"Ryoma, come here for a minute."

"Okay."

"First up, good work today. Today's pile of monster corpses is in the usual spot. With the completion of this job, you've been moved up to E rank. Also... I heard from the duke's butler that you're going to be managing this mine?"

"Yes, that's right."

"I'm sure you'll be fine, but be careful. If you're short on hands, speak up anytime. Reporting that is your job too, got it?"

"Got it."

"At any rate, I really am impressed by your determination for independence from the duke's house."

"I realized I was being spoiled too much by them, so I thought I'd pull myself together."

"You're still a kid, so don't push yourself. Actually, about that... is it true you're running a laundry service with your cleaner slimes for that purpose?"

"It's true. Did you hear about it already?"

"It's been spread quite a lot between the adventurers on this job, y'know? Seems like they're all waiting for it to open. Most of them have piles of dirty clothes left lying around."

"I'm glad to hear that. I'll move faster constructing the store, so please wait a little longer."

"Right. There's one more thing I wanted to ask — could I use the service too? And how much does it cost?"

"Of course, anyone is free to use it. The cost is 1 medium bronze coin per bag, which is provided by the store. There are also two options for groups, which involve a discounted service."

"Oh? Then I'll gather the guild employees and ask if anyone else is interested... How much of a benefit will it be, speaking frankly?"

"Comparing the cost of one week's worth of clothes between the individual option and the largest group option, it'd be approximately 20% cheaper."

"By that much?"

f"It was originally a job I came up with to earn the minimum living costs I needed between adventurer jobs, so I intended on making it cheap. The discount isn't limited to first-time customers and will be applied every time for groups, so it'd be a benefit to use the service as a guild."

"In that case, I'll have to talk to others even more."

"Thank you for your consideration."

Our conversation ended there, and I returned to town to finish demolishing the building.

Because the job at the mines ended before lunch, I still had time leftover after finishing all the weeding and demolition. The land foundations were still good, so now I had to decide on a building...

It was at this point that my gaze wandered to the front of the land, where I noticed several children were watching me.

"Do you need something?"

I called out to them gently, and a particularly young boy among the group answered.

"Never seen you before! Who are you, anyway?!"

"Hey, Rick! Don't be rude!"

The hostile words made a girl standing next to the young boy scold him, and the oldest-looking boy bowed his head instead.

"Sorry for that. Rick is a bit of a brat. And sorry for disturbing your work."

"Oh no, I was so focused that I didn't notice at all. I'm almost done anyway, so it's not a problem."

Rather than that, I was more curious about these children's ages.

Were they children? Could they be like that adventurer group, where the smallest was actually the oldest?

"Really? Thanks. You seem cool. You don't look that much different in age to me, yet you can use magic so well."

"Are you a magician, mister?"

"An adventurer?"

The group of kids fired one question after another. Their carefree and outspoken questions were a little overwhelming, but I would do my best to answer — when a woman's voice called over them first.

"Calm down! The poor boy can't answer if you all ask at once!"

I looked in the direction of the voice to see a woman of good physique standing there.

"Sorry if the children were bothering you."

"They weren't a bother at all, but thank you."

"Hmm, you seem rather polite for your age. I wish my son would be the same. Are you an adventurer?"

"Yes, I registered just the other day."

"I see. Well, do your best. Are you here on some job today? This empty lot's looking clean for the first time in ages."

"No, I'm preparing to open a laundry service here... Ah, sorry. My name is Ryoma Takebayashi."

"I'm Pauline. This cheeky one is my son Rick, and that tomboy is my daughter Renny."

"I'm Rick, currently accepting henchmen!"

"What kind of rubbish are you on about?! Sorry about him, I'm Renny. Nice to meet you."

"I'm Thor, hello."

"It's a pleasure to meet you, I'm Ryoma Takebayashi. Are you all locals of this neighborhood?"

"Yeah, both these kids and my kids live in the residential area over there. And I own the florist next door."

"Oh, then that makes us next-door neighbors. I'll pay you a proper visit at a later date, so I hope we can get along in the future."

"It's fine, don't worry about that. Anyways, did you mention a laundry service? Will you wash clothes for money?"

"Yes."

I took out one of the individual sized bags from my Item Box and gave a simple explanation.

"This is the bag for single households. It'll cost 1 medium bronze for a bag of this size to be washed."

When I said that, Pauline expressed her interest.

"1 medium bronze for this? That's cheaper than I expected."

"If you'd like, I can give you a free trial once the store is open. Since we're next-door neighbors."

"Really? Then I'll take you up on that offer."

After that, I asked her about the local area before thanking her and going home.

⤚ Chapter 2 Episode 23 ⤙
Store Setup 2

Store Construction, Day 3.

As a result of thinking all night at the inn, I determined that a two-story building with a basement was the limit of my architecture skill. Thus, I would experimentally use my architecture skill to its limit and construct a two-story building with a basement.

However, there was too much land to dedicate entirely to the storefront, so I decided half would be for the store, a quarter would be for employee dorms, and the remaining quarter would be a backyard.

I planned the land for the storefront with Create Block, simultaneously digging the basement and creating stone material. The completed bricks were transported by the slimes to be stored.

With the whole that was created from that work, I used my architecture skill to create the earth magic Pavement, reinforcing the ground into a solid foundation. It was like compressing the ground and hardening it, removing any cracks until it became a single flat layer of stone. This way, it was like completing the foundation works on Earth of macadam, leveling concrete, and base concrete at once.

In Japan, there was a step in-between leveling concrete and base concrete to place bar reinforcement, but there was no construction knowledge of that in this world. Was that okay? It made me worry about earthquakes… Was it unnecessary in places without earthquakes?

My knowledge of Earth architecture ended at my part-time job experience, and there was no knowledge of it in this world. For now, all the foundation work used in this world was done… It should be good enough for now, and I didn't want to ruin anything with my vague knowledge.

I stacked the stone blocks from earlier up, using the sticky slime's hardening solution in place of concrete, which hardened for more reinforcement. This work didn't require magic, so I asked the slimes to help too and steadily progressed until I could put up stone pillars with magic. The basement and its walls, the first floor base and outer walls of the store were done.

Magic was truly convenient. I hadn't used any wood or a single sute up until here. It was a simple build consisting of a stone box with stone pillars and reinforced walls, but it should be more than sturdy enough.

Everything was going so smoothly that, for a second, I played around with the idea of creating ancient temple pillars like those I had seen in my school textbooks, but I stopped. There was no need to make the basement that extravagant.

I've used a fair bit of magic already, so I should wrap it up for today…

Store Construction, Day 4.

On the base of the first floor, I divided sections for rooms with hardening solution and stone bricks. Then, I made the second floor, which took up the whole day.

■ ■ ■

Store Construction, Day 5.

I created the ceiling and furnished the interior. Then, after cutting down some of the trees near the mines, I used my woodworking skill knowledge to process wood with magic.

With alchemy, I could slowly draw the moisture out of the wood. Then, I applied the wind magic Windcutter to imitate lumber processing on Earth by developing a new magic called Circle Saw. I then mixed wind magic and earth magic to create Polish Wheel to further refine the planks that were created.

The spell worked by using Break Rock to create sand and spin it around Circle Saw like a tire. Instead of slicing things, the magic would use the rapidly rotating sand within the wind to polish the surface of an object.

Many of the wood that was dried by alchemy had bends in it from where the moisture was removed. But, well, since it wasn't being used for pillars, it should be fine.

Processing the wood and planks took a whole day in itself…

■ ■ ■

Store Construction, Day 6.

Using the wooden materials prepared yesterday, I created shelves and counters. Afterward, I used sticky solution as a replacement for varnish, coating them before letting them dry. I covered the walls and floor with planks too. A stone building gave a rather gloomy feeling for a shop.

I used earth magic to adjust things until the interior had a more wooden feel to it, at which point I noticed the cleaner slimes were acting weird.

Were they eating the sawdust from my work? They ate filth, but they never usually ate rubbish on their own… If they were scavenger slimes, maybe… Hmm? They weren't eating it, but gathering it together and spitting it all out in one spot? …They were cleaning?!

I hurriedly used Monster Appraisal on the cleaner slimes to find they had a new level-1 skill called Cleanup. I had no idea such a skill existed — was it even a skill a slime could learn? …Well, it was a bit late to question that. Some had already learned pole mastery.

When I checked the other slimes out of curiosity, an acid slime had level 1 in woodworking.

All I did was give it some simple tasks in helping with the demolished building's wooden rubble, holding a tool to chip away at the wood, and using its acid to melt wooden materials for simple processing… Was this all it took to learn skills in this world?

…Well, who cared as long as I made progress? Yeah, let's leave it at that.

After that, I chopped some planks and left the adjustment of size and shapes to the acid slime, increasing my work efficiency even more. Seeing the resulting wood, it seemed like the acid slime could do a surprisingly good job.

■　■　■

Store Construction, Day 7.

The interior of the customer-facing section was done. All that was left was the exterior. It wouldn't impact business to have blocks the color of hardened dirt, but I wanted to apply some treatment to it. A laundry service was a kind of cleaning shop… The first color that came to mind was white. If possible, I wanted the outer walls to be white, or at least a cleaner color than dirt.

This was something even I couldn't fix through magic, so I decided to visit Serge and ask about it.

"So you want to make the walls white…"

"Is that doable?"

"It is, but it's uncommon to do that for a business. It's mostly used for mansions belonging to the nobility, as white stone is expensive and any dirt on the surface would stand out."

"That's true… but I don't think the current color of the outer walls is ideal for a laundry service. Wouldn't a white wall feel more sanitary than the color of dirt?"

"Indeed it would. I definitely agree with you there. But we don't have much stock of it, either."

It was a bit late for it now, but I should have gone to a carpenter or engineering firm if I wanted assistance with construction. Actually, why did he have any stock at all?

"Our Morgan Trading Company prides itself on its product lineup. Even if there's no stock, we are able to obtain most items if given enough time."

Which meant I could order things too, huh? But I spent a lot of money buying the land already… Come to think of it, wasn't this town a mining town with iron mines?

"Mr. Serge, this town has an ironworks, right?"

"That it does, but how will that help?"

"If there's an ironworks, then does that mean they use lime in their iron manufacturing?"

"You are well informed. Indeed, lime is used."

"Is it possible to obtain that lime? For a cheap price, if possible."

"It is. My stores also carry it in stock, and it isn't a very expensive product to begin with."

"Great. Then perhaps I could harden the lime into white stone material."

Lime was a building material used in Japan for plaster too. There was no issue with the color, either. While I didn't know how to make plaster, I could just turn it into blocks with magic. If I coated it in sticky slime solution, it'd be protected from rain and dirt as well.

That idea hadn't occurred to Serge, who immediately went to prepare the lime. It could be transformed into slaked lime with alchemy and water, and could be refined into blocks from a single lump.

Serge seemed interested in the aspect of a cheap white stone material, but I made myself scarce after buying a large sack of lime. He was a good person, but I wanted to focus on my store first.

I returned to the store and silently worked at producing stone bricks to paste on the walls. I had finished covering the house as the sun was starting to set, and after I hardened the gaps with magic and lime I called upon all my sticky slimes. Then the sticky solution coating on the white exterior was complete.

There was still a fair bit of lime left, which I stored in my Dimension Home for now.

"It's coming together well."

My rushed construction was generally done. But this time, with how white the store was, its appearance started to look a little lonely.

I would have liked to plant some lawn so that the exposed dirt could be hidden, but...

...Come to think of it, the next-door neighbors were florists. They might sell seeds.

With haste, I headed over. As I stood outside the store, a voice could be heard.

"Welcome! Ah, it's Ryoma!"

"Hello… Renny."

I couldn't remember her name for a second.

"There's no need for any of that. I'm younger than you, just talk to me however. So, what's up?"

"Okay, Renny. I want to buy flowers or grass seeds."

"Seeds? We have several types. One sec. Mom!"

Renny yelled into the store loudly, where Pauline was talking to two women at the counter.

"Don't yell; it's terribly impolite."

"I'm only yelling 'cause you won't stop talking, Mom! And you have a customer!"

"Oh, if it isn't Ryoma. Did you come to buy something?"

"My, is this Ryoma?"

"He's so tiny; how impressive."

The two women who were chatting with Pauline came along too.

"Hello, I'm Ryoma Takebayashi."

"Oh my, how polite indeed. I'd love for my child to learn a thing or two like that. I'm Kiara, nice to meet you."

"I'm Mary, it's a pleasure to see you. I've heard the rumors."

"Rumors?"

"You've been building your store next door for a few days in a row now, yes? It's come together so well, everyone's been talking about how you're a master magician."

"I only use lifestyle-related magic, really, so I just happened to be good at this kind of work."

"That's more than remarkable already, if you can build such a sturdy looking building. The rumors also say you keep a large number of slimes."

"That would be the truth."

"We know; we've seen it with our own eyes."

"There were an amazing number of slimes carrying the blocks you made."

"You saw that?"

"It was my first time seeing slimes move like that. I couldn't help but stare."

"Tamers aren't rare to see in Gimul Town, but their monsters are all terrifying. Oops, you were here to shop. What did you need?"

"Do you have any flower or grass seeds?"

"I do. The flower seeds will vary in cost based on their type, but grass seeds are 130 sutes a bag. How much do you need?"

"I'd like to plant a lawn around the store I just built..."

I tried calculating how much I would need, which Pauline saw and offered to help with.

"Could you show me around your store? I can give you some advice."

"Thank you so much."

I led Pauline over, trailed by Renny, Kiara, and Mary. Guess everyone was coming along for the ride.

The four of them stopped when they saw my store and examined it carefully.

"Is something the matter?"

"I'm surprised. Was the store this color this morning?"

"I repainted it just now. I thought a dirt-colored store didn't seem clean enough for a store offering a laundry service, so I bought lime and worked on it with some magic and slimes."

"Huh... you really work fast."

"This does look much cleaner."

"A laundry service, you say? Perhaps I'll try it out as well. If I could save on laundry, I'd have more time for other housework."

"Please come and try it. Since we've just become new acquaintances, I'll give you a free trial."

I took out two bags from my Item Box and gave them one each. I had to secure customers where I could!

After that, I had Pauline make a selection for me and purchased 15 bags of grass seeds and two bags each of four types of flowers. I'd start planting them tomorrow.

Speaking of which, who was it that told me I could put an advertisement up on the guild bulletin board again...?

I should visit the guild tomorrow, for the sake of my scavenger slimes making fertilizer as well.

With that decided, it was time to go home and think about the ad details!

～ Chapter 2 Episode 24 ～
Store Setup 3

"Hmm…"

After returning to the inn, I began thinking about the advertisement. But there was one thing I couldn't quite settle on. The name of the shop. I couldn't come up with anything clever…

As I was painstakingly pondering over it, Sebas dropped by.

"Have you returned, Master Ryoma?"

"Yes, I'm here."

"Master Ryoma, my lady would like to invite you to have tea together."

"That sounds nice. I just hit a dead end with my work anyway. I shall gratefully accept."

It would be a good change of pace.

"I've been waiting, Ryoma."

"Please have a seat."

"Thank you very much."

I took a sip of the tea that was served, which was when Reinhart asked, "Seems like you've been working hard lately. You haven't been pushing yourself, have you?"

"No, I'm fine."

"How's your work coming along?"

"The store's almost done. All that's left to do tomorrow is to plant some grass and flowers around the store, grow them with wood magic, then make some billboards and signs."

"Huh?! You've already completed that much?!"

"Ryoma, have you actually been pushing yourself?"

"No, not in particular."

"Master Ryoma, I heard that you were building with earth magic. How much magic energy do you think you're using every day?"

"Let me think… I use it until just before the symptoms of magic fatigue show up. The rest I do by hand, if I can."

At my words, everyone other than me sighed.

"That's already more than enough…"

"Master Ryoma's level of magic fatigue could easily knock out a royal sorcerer. The amount of work you could do alone would definitely count as working too hard."

Come to think of it, I had an irregularly high amount of magic energy.

"Your face says you've only just realized it."

"I suddenly feel rather concerned. Will you really be okay alone…?"

"I'll be fine. It's nothing compared to my old workplace."

"What did you do at your old workplace?"

"Huh…?"

I had spoken without thinking, but I couldn't tell them I was a software engineer or programmer… I guess I could talk about my part-time gigs.

"I did all kinds of things… Everything from cargo transportation to making dolls."

"I see… Did you ever find your work grueling?"

"There were times that I did, but if I didn't work I wouldn't have been able to survive… And it wasn't like everything was grueling. The cargo transportation I mentioned was for materials at a construction site, and it was intriguing to see the construction come together. I felt a sense of accomplishment when it was completed, too. Dollmaking involved adding designated colors to designated locations, which was repetitive, but it made me happy to see the completed product."

"I see. I hope I'll find work that's worth doing in the future too."

Huh, was Eliaria going to work? Even though she was the daughter of a Duke?

As I was wondering that, Eliaria expressed interest in the dollmaking. So she did have a girlish side...

"I could make one for you sometime, if you'd like?"

Without thinking too deeply, I ran my mouth on the spur of the moment. The dolls I made were all targeted for boys.

"Really?! If you have the time, then please!"

...Oh no! This was bad news on so many levels! I made many things for a hobby and for profit, but the people here wouldn't understand the material. And making something unsuitable for Eliaria's age was out of the question...

"Is something the matter?"

"No, it's just... The modeling... I was in charge of applying colors, so now that I think about it, I don't have a base..."

"Oh? But Ryoma, you're good at earth magic."

...That was true. The convenience of earth magic was now my downfall...

Well, no helping that, I guess. I was the one who made the offer, so I'll just make something appropriately harmless.

"I understand. I shall make it when I have the time."

"Thank you."

"Sebas, where can I buy art supplies like paints and things?"

"If you're in need, I can prepare some by tomorrow."

"Thank you. I need some for my store signs too, so please prepare extra. I'll pay you for it later."

"Understood."

After that, we chatted idly for a while before I returned to my room. When I was leaving, they emphasized how I shouldn't be pushing myself too hard... I should be careful.

Oh yeah, what was I going to do about the store name?

...

...

...

...

...Something simple would be enough. Being easy to remember was important too.

Bamboo Forest Laundry Service — Filthy Cleans at a Reasonable Price! We Can Even Handle Goblin Filth!

Yeah, the literal translation of my name would be pretty easy to recall. This would do nicely for an ad.

■ ■ ■

Store Construction, Day 8.

I received the art supplies from Sebas and thanked him before heading to the guild, where I was hailed down by the receptionist Maylene.

"Oh, if it isn't Ryoma! You stopped showing up at the guild after the job at the mines, so I was worried."

"Sorry, I've been rather busy."

"That's right, you're building a store. I heard about it from the guildmaster. Quite impressive for your age."

"Thank you very much. Actually, I had something to ask about."

"Go on."

"I heard somewhere that I could post an ad to the guild bulletin board; is that true?"

"Ads? Hmm, the guild doesn't have that kind of service. What you heard about was probably that."

Maylene pointed to a small bulletin board in the corner of the guild.

"It's a bulletin board for people seeking parties. People who want party members can write about themselves and what they're seeking. There's no bulletin board for shop advertisements, though."

"I see... Thank you."

I guess this meant I'd have to work on promoting myself through word of mouth? Passing out flyers and sticking up posters seemed like a rather expensive option because of the cost of paper, though...

The only exception was toilet paper, which was pretty much free to use. Apparently there had been a man in the past (most likely an otherworlder) who created magic tools that produced toothbrushes and toilet paper, then spread it throughout the world. But I couldn't use toilet paper to write my ads on.

It was definitely too frail, and would just be thrown away. I should set aside the store for now and get to work.

"Miss Maylene, are there any jobs for cleaning rubbish or the likes today?"

"If it's about that, could you visit the guildmaster's office? He wanted to talk to you the next time you dropped by, so it's probably about a job."

"I understand. I'll be off now."

When I went to the guildmaster's office, he welcomed me with a bright smile.

"Ryoma! You're finally here!"

"Hello. Has it been around a week? I was completely occupied with my store setup."

"Sorry to spring this upon you, but I'd like you to accept another toilet-cleaning job."

What? I thought the six slum kids were taking care of those...

"About that... the six kids you mentioned and some others have stepped up, but we're still short on hands. We've made some of Sacchi's lot — the ones with lighter punishments — take on the job too, but it's still not enough. And their work just isn't as good as yours. While I would love to give the jobs to those without money... as a guild, it isn't good to keep our clients waiting for too long. The five months before you arrived were pretty tough. We're all sick of that stench from back then! Even the smell was gone for a period of time! Make it that clean again! ...And those are just some of the complaints we get from short-tempered people. Please, just as much as we're short on is fine."

Yikes... Did I make it too clean? Did raising the bar on quality of life make it harder to return to normal? ...While I'm sure that was part of it, those five months must have been really tough...

"Well, I can understand their reasoning. That stench really was terrible... I shall take on the job."

"That would be great."

I immediately accepted the request and headed for the toilet pits.

Making the most use out of my scavenger slimes finished the job in no time at all.

All that was left was to report the job completion and accept the reward. Then it was back to store work.

I asked my scavenger slimes to use their nutrient reduction skill to take the nutrients from their food and spit it out as fertilizer. I mixed the scentless mud into the dirt around the store and planted the grass and flower seeds, watering them after.

"It's gotten dark..."

Because the cleaning job had taken some time, the sun was starting to set.

I was told not to work too hard just yesterday... Guess I should leave it here for today.

■　■　■

Store Construction, Day 9.

In the morning, I watered the grass and flower seeds I planted with water magic, then used the wood magic Grow to accelerate their growth. Three hours after casting the magic, there was a fresh green lawn around the store perimeter and flowers blooming everywhere.

This magic was useful, but if there wasn't enough nutrients and water in the soil then more magic energy would be expended instead, and it also had the demerit of sapping out all the nutrients in the soil if used for excessively rapid growth. If it hadn't been for the scavenger slimes' fertilizer, even I wouldn't have had enough magic energy to allow such a wide area of lawn to grow in such a short time.

It was all well that I succeeded... Once I clipped the lawn to an appropriate length with wind magic and let the scavenger slimes eat the grass clippings, the exterior preparations would be complete. Next, I would finally move on to preparing the shop's face — the sign.

I took one of the planks of wood I had cut and painted it white, then wrote *Bamboo Forest Laundry Service* on it. After drawing some bamboo thickets and slimes on both sides, I set it aside to dry. All that was left was to apply a waterproof coat to it and it would be complete.

While it dried, I went about making the sign of the laundry fees and everything else, then made my final checks on the store.

Next was… checking the flow of management and contact with customers?

In which case, I should open the store and call Jeff and the others to test it out… No, I should just make it an opening party!

There was no time like the present. I made sure I had the minimum preparations needed to open the business, then dropped by Serge's place on my way home.

"Welcome, Master Ryoma."

"Good evening, Mr. Serge. To get straight down to business, as of today I've completed the store."

"Really?! That was rather fast…"

"Some acquaintances at the Adventurer's Guild told me they were eagerly awaiting the opening of my store, so I've been putting some effort into getting it done. Now that I've managed to get everything in shape, I'd like to call them over for an opening party, but I want to confirm that everything is in order for the business to open."

"So a final confirmation before opening for real?"

"Yes. I'll open to the public the day after that, so I was thinking of preparing an opening party with a light meal. I was hoping to invite Mr. Serge too, so if you're interested in coming, could you let me know your available days?"

"Thank you for the invitation. Let me see… I have some things to do tomorrow, but I don't have any plans in the two weeks after that. Anytime convenient for you works for me."

"Thank you very much. I'll check with my acquaintances and let you know my decision."

"Master Ryoma, could I bring two people along with me to that party?"

"Sure. Is it Mr. Pioro and the guildmaster?"

"No, they're from my trading company. I previously promised to introduce you to some shop assistants. It would benefit them too to become more familiar with the work earlier."

"Thank you for the consideration."

Come to think of it, he had mentioned that before. After making the lodgings for the employees, I forgot about them. I wouldn't be able to work as an adventurer if I was on my own, so it was a fairly important point. Thank goodness.

I expressed my appreciation once more and left the store.

Next, I went to the Adventurer's Guild and asked the guildmaster and Maylene the same thing. The two of them had a day off in three days' time. They would also tell Jeff and everyone from the epidemic prevention team for me. I should drop by the guild again tomorrow.

After that, I went to the Merchant's Guild and asked the receptionist to pass on a message to the guildmaster, when they let me through to see her instead.

"Welcome, it's been a little over a week since then. Has everything been progressing smoothly?"

"Fortunately, I've been able to put the store together."

"Already? Well, it depends on the building, but you could also make a good carpenter, eh?"

"I can only construct a simple building, though."

"That's more than enough. Only nobles and oddballs want extravagant homes."

I guess that made sense.

"Did you come to report your store completion today?"

"That, and I'd like to gather the people I know to take on some jobs and confirm that the business procedure is functioning correctly. After that, I wanted to hold an opening party with a light meal. I've been in your care too, Guildmaster, so if you're available…"

"You're inviting me?"

"I can't prepare anything extravagant, and my other acquaintances will be there too. But if you're willing to come, you're most welcome to."

"Heehee! I can think of it as a casual feast then, yes? That makes me happy. With my position, I'm rarely ever invited to gatherings. Even when they call it a casual gathering, sometimes I arrive and everyone's all stiff as boards. But if they're your adventurer friends, it really will be a casual gathering, hmm?"

"Yes, I also dislike formal social events. They're just places to watch your words and actions."

"All right, when is it?"

"I'm thinking in three days from now, but the final decision will be made after I hear the responses from everyone else… I'll leave a message at the guild tomorrow. Also, could you tell me how to contact Mr. Pioro? I'd like to invite him too, if he has the time."

"His schedule should be completely open three days from now. He's headquartered in another town, you see, but he'll be here tomorrow for the meeting. I'll make sure to let him know."

"Thank you very much."

I thanked her and left the Merchant's Guild.

Finally, I dropped by the Tamer's Guild before heading back to the inn and invited Eliaria and everyone to the pre-opening of the store and the opening party. They were all delighted to hear that, and the four members of the ducal family, Sebas, Araune, Lilianne, and Jill and the other escorts all agreed to come.

With that, the number of attendees totaled 11 from Eliaria's group, 11 from the Adventurer's Guild and 5 from the Merchant's Guild... which made 28 people, including me. With no real achievements, I hadn't been able to meet Branch Head Taylor today to receive his reply, but if he could come, that would make 29. The opening party would have to be held in the employee break room, that area should be wide enough.

Tomorrow I would confirm the plans of the adventurers and contact everyone else.

Day 10.

After visiting the guild, I confirmed that all of the invited adventurers were attending. Furthermore, the message I left at the Tamer's Guild yesterday was passed on properly, and I received a reply that Branch Head Taylor was attending too.

As soon as I heard that, I went to Serge's store and informed him that the trial run would happen in the morning two days from now, and the opening party would be at lunch.

All that was left was to patrol the abandoned mines that I had neglected for the past week and clean out any monsters there before heading back to the inn and informing Eliaria and the others about the plans.

∽ Chapter 2 Episode 25 ∽
Store Setup 4

Day 11.

In the morning, I ran around purchasing a large amount of ingredients and used my time to prepare what dishes I could today.

The menu for tomorrow was spaghetti with meat sauce, steak, and salad. And an apple pie for dessert.

I had pondered over what to serve, but pasta and steak existed in this world too. It should be a safe option to go with. Though it wasn't very party-like. The first party food that came to my mind was pizza, but I was yet to see it in this world so I decided against it.

For drinks, there was water, booze, and two types of fruit juice.

Since it was a celebration, I splurged a little on the alcohol and purchased the shop assistant's recommendation for 30 peoples' worth at a budget of 3 small gold, and the fruit juice was homemade.

For the cooking, my alchemy came in unexpectedly handy. For example, after making the spaghetti noodles, I could use alchemy to separate the moisture from it and instantly create dehydrated noodles. That meant all I had to do tomorrow was boil it. For the fruit juice, I could separate the fruit pulp from the liquid to make 100% fruit juice.

Was it really okay to use alchemy in this way?

Finally... when I made meat sauce in my past life, I would always use premade sauces sold on the shelves, but that wasn't available here. So I decided to make a vegetable and poultry soup today. Then, if I mince the meat I bought today and fry it with tomatoes tomorrow, I can add it to the soup to make a similar-tasting sauce.

The completed dishes were placed in a wooden box coated with the sticky slime's hardening solution, then within a barrier that was originally meant for keeping the cold out, but reversed so that it would keep the cold in.

For the record, when I appraised this contraption it showed up as a single item called a cooler box, along with information about the specific contents and how close to going bad they were. It was extremely impressive, but rather than calling it an effect of the cooler box, it was more like one of the clever functions of appraisal magic.

Once I finished cooking, it was just before evening.

It was a bit too late to go to the guild now, so maybe I should go home…?

I wandered the town like that, until I spotted the church.

Oh yeah, I haven't prayed in a while. I should go and make a prayer.

I turned my feet towards the church on a whim and was greeted by a girl in her teens.

"Welcome to the church. What are you here for today?"

"I had some free time, so I'd like to offer a prayer to the gods."

"In that case, please come this way."

I was led to a room with many chairs lined before an altar. Apparently I was free to pray all I wanted here. The girl told me to take my time before leaving the room.

There wasn't much else I could do… I thought, sitting in a nearby seat before clasping my hands together and closing my eyes.

Several seconds later.

I felt like something was slipping out of my body, but it wasn't a bad sensation.

When I opened my eyes... I was in the pure white scenery I had witnessed twice before.

"Did I come here again...?"

"Yup, you're here again."

I turned around at the sound of that voice to see Kufo.

"Nice to see you again, Kufo."

"Long time no see! But not that long, it's only been a month since last time."

"Are Gain and Lulutia not here?"

"Yup. They've stepped out for a bit."

"Huh, gods can step out?"

"It's not that uncommon of an event."

"Wow. Where did they go?"

At my question, Kufo made a face of sudden regret.

"Ah... Umm... Actually, they went to your old world."

"To Earth?! But why? To bring someone over?"

"No no! It's not like that, not this time..."

Kufo struggled for words.

"This time? If you can't say it then I won't ask anymore, but..."

"Mm... I guess it's okay if it's you? They went sightseeing."

"Excuse me?"

Sightseeing?

"Lulutia is going on a sweets tour of your world, while Gain is currently into one of Japan's idol groups."

"What kind of reason is that?! Though it's fine by me... but are they allowed to cross worlds so freely?"

"Generally speaking, gods can't interfere with each other's worlds. But we've been interacting by taking people and magic energy from Earth for a long time now... and there aren't many forms of entertainment in this world, you see. Even Lulutia's tour is because of the lack of dessert variety in this world, not to mention how they all taste bad in comparison to your world's."

"Well, I guess that's true."

"I went around the Earth's secluded regions recently, too. As a god of life, I had a look at all the living beings living in harsh environments. Like in the Amazon, the Sahara Desert, Atlantis, and the deep sea."

"Hey, there's something strange mixed in there?!"

"Keep this a secret from the other humans, okay? Our dignity as gods is on the line."

"Don't just ignore me. And no one would believe me anyway…"

"I suppose that's true."

Kufo cackled with childish laughter.

If the scale of his words hadn't been so tremendous, I would've forgotten he was a god.

"But Gain aside, wouldn't it be fine if you spread more of the sweets Lulutia likes in this world? There are lots of otherworlders here, no?"

"While you have a point, it's difficult for cooking recipes to spread here. There's nothing convenient like the Earth's internet in this world, and sugar and spices can't be obtained easily either. You know how foods with many spices are considered high-class items, right?"

"Oh, that's true."

"There are several things that have been handed down as luxuries of royalty and nobility, but commoners don't have access to the ingredients for them. That's why otherworlders who come here don't have the ingredients to recreate the tastes of their home, and those that do have trouble passing those recipes on to future generations. For example… you recently met a person named Pioro Saionji, right?"

"I did. I thought Saionji sounded like a family name; was he a descendant of an otherworlder after all?"

"Yup. The otherworlder was the son of an okonomiyaki store-owner, a student that was enrolled in a specialty school for cooking. He tried to make okonomiyaki in this world, but he couldn't make the sauce and didn't have the seafood needed, so he traveled the world gathering ingredients. He funded his travels and ingredient fees by opening stalls on his journey and making a killing. As a result, he managed to make okonomiyaki to a satisfactory degree, but it didn't spread. Then, he used the personal connections and culinary knowledge he gained on his path to making okonomiyaki to form a guild that focused on dealing in foodstuffs. That's the origin story of the current Saionji Trading Company. To put it another way, ingredients were so difficult to source in the time period he lived in, he could only recreate okonomiyaki after traveling the world and forming a guild. Nowadays there's the Saionji Company and those that imitated it, so foodstuffs have become a little easier to obtain."

So that was what happened...

"This kind of story doesn't only apply to food, but other things too. Techniques, knowledge, anything. Not all otherworlders had passion like him — some had the motivation but no ability or knowledge, and many were just unlucky. There are some arts that were lost due to war or interference from other otherworlders too."

"When you put it that way, it makes sense. But what do you mean by interference from other otherworlders? Did they bring in a better technique?"

"...I can only call it bad luck. A long time ago, there was a medical student who came to this world and spread the knowledge of medicine and disease. But there's nothing like that around anymore, right?"

"Yeah, the guildmaster didn't know anything about epidemics either."

"Actually, the person who came before the last person before you... said she wanted to be a saint."

"A saint? A holy figure worshiped in churches?"

"Yup, that's the one. One with a mysterious power that can heal others, yeah. She wanted to do things like that and have people fawn over her. But she wasn't a bad person. She wanted to be the center of attention, but she also wanted to help other people. That's why Lulutia, Gain, and I gave her our protection. She couldn't resurrect the dead but she could heal any injury or disease, was immune to poison and drugs, and had protection preventing sickness, harm, and being restrained. She intended on living her life as a saint that way, but..."

"But?"

What could have happened?

"She could heal any disease, but because everyone else could only use regular healing magic, they couldn't heal diseases. At the time, there were diseases that couldn't be treated with the medical science of this world, so those people would die unless they were treated by her. When she saw that, she realized those types of deaths would increase after she was gone... As a result, at the end of her life she gave up everything to use the divine power of the gods. To erase all disease from this world."

"Erase all disease from the world?! How can that be possible?"

"It isn't possible. Not normally, at least. But, because she was an otherworlder that had directly received our power, and the fact she had gathered so many believers with her achievements until then, the prayers of all those people amplified her power and gave it a boost. To put it simply, she cheated the system. And she really did give up everything for it. After she used the power, she passed away and her soul was extinguished. Normally one would be reincarnated, but she even used up that power and disappeared."

"She's... kind of amazing..."

"She wanted to be a saint out of admiration and had some trouble at the start, but her sense of duty and everything led her to become a real saint in every meaning of the word in the end.

Changing the energy of prayers into power is something natural for us, but... As a result of her actions, people lived practically disease-free for nearly 400 years in this world. Injuries still happened so healing magic remained, but knowledge about disease and medicines to heal them were lost over time, leading to the current state of things. The effects of her actions are gone now, but the lost knowledge won't return."

"I see..."

Still, it was hard to believe that one person could do such a thing. It really was like a cheat...

"Ah, as long as you're willing to give up your soul, you could probably do something similar. Just not to the same extent."

"Seriously?!"

"When you combine a human soul with a god's power, you can create a pretty powerful force. That's what allows us to use your soul to bring magic energy into this world from another world. Although, if you tried to do the same thing as her, you would only be able to erase all disease for a few years at most. In her case, she was surrounded by believers and specialized in healing so it held out for 400 years, but you have no worshipers and your abilities are all balanced. As a result, you have practically no limits to your growth and the speed of your growth is also fast, so with time you have the potential to become stronger than anyone. And the best part is — it's fun for us to watch too!"

"That's your conclusion?"

"But there's nothing else to do in the divine realm!"

Just as Kufo said that, light started glowing around us. That sure looked familiar.

"Looks like our time's up."

"Huh, already? ...Oh, I see! Gain and Lulutia aren't here, so the time you can remain here on my power alone is shortened... Ryoma!"

"What? There's no rush..."

"I had something to tell you when I called you here! I've wasted all our time chatting, so let me get to the point! We forgot to tell you this, but your mind is being influenced by your younger body and experiencing a slight infantile regression! The same happened to other otherworlders too! You may have lived for over 30 years on Earth before dying as Takebayashi Ryoma, but you're 11-year-old Ryoma Takebayashi here! That's why you can't always control yourself or maintain a poker face! You can try to train yourself over again, but don't push yourself too hard!"

After Kufo said that in a panic, light filled my vision and returned me to the previous room I was in.

What did he mean? My mind was being influenced by my body? I didn't get it, but... it sounded kind of important?

I could kind of understand the infantile regression... When I worked at the company in my previous life, I was often told no one could see through my poker face. But now I'm often told my thoughts are written all over my face. That was something I was told often as a kid, too... Well, that didn't change what I was doing, but since Kufo went out of his way to tell me that, I'll keep it in mind.

I thanked Kufo in my heart, gave a small donation and left the church.

It was starting to get dark, so I returned to the inn for today.

Everyone was coming to the store tomorrow. I should rest early and work hard!

⋟ **Extra Story** ⋞
The Ones Left Behind and the Signs of Change

"TABUCHI! Is Takebayashi still absent?!"

"Y-Yes, sir!"

"Any contact?!"

"None yet! I can't get ahold of him, either!"

"Well, keep trying! A client contacted us about being stood up for a meeting!"

"How is that my problem, exactly…"

"Fuck you, you insubordinate prick! If you've got that much time to dick around, then call him! If he's not coming in, you do his work! Am I making myself crystal fucking clear?!"

"Y-Yes, sir!"

"Then move! Christ… bunch of useless pansies. Hopeless people like him are always pushing the burden onto the rest of us."

"If that ain't the truth."

"And this is supposed to be my senior? You gotta be kidding."

"So, like, is the chief AWOL?"

"Dunno. Who cares about that old man."

"But like, we should at least give him a call. He should know how to act like an adult at his age."

"He's definitely fired after this. Reckon they'll let him in tomorrow?"

"…"

A boss that yelled irrationally. Tabuchi, being yelled at irrationally. The young coworkers who watched on and laughed scornfully.

The other employees that worked silently alongside.

They held their tongues, letting sleeping dogs lie as they quietly hoped for Ryoma's return.

But on this day, Ryoma did not appear in the office.

Because of that…

"Damn it. Why do I have to do this?"

"…"

On a train before the rush hour home, a clearly displeased man and Tabuchi stood together.

"Iguchi, this is inside the carriage…"

The man was hogging a senior seat that happened to be empty and grumbling about his discontent in a loud and self-important voice.

The other passengers couldn't have felt comfortable riding with a person with that attitude.

"Huh? Shut up. It's not like it's packed or anything."

Tabuchi's words couldn't appease Iguchi. Instead, he was glared at.

"…What the hell are you looking at, bitch?"

"Iguchi!"

They must have accidentally made eye contact. He looked at the two middle-aged women who were clearly showing discomfort, but Tabuchi stepped in before he stood up.

"Let's go."

"Yes, let's…"

"…"

It seemed like he had noticed that he was gathering attention from not only Tabuchi and the women moving to the next carriage, but the rest of the carriage too. Iguchi cast his sharp glare across the carriage, then snorted when he saw the passengers avert their gaze.

"How long are you gonna stand there for? Move it! You're suffocating me, you fat fuck."

"Sorry."

"Tell me when we arrive."

Iguchi shoved away Tabuchi, who had been standing before him, then took out a music player from his pocket and started listening to music. Seeing him made Tabuchi think to himself.

There has to be some abuse going on to choose him… isn't there?

His boss had ordered him to make sure Ryoma was at the office tomorrow, even if he had to drag him there. But if all that was needed was a visit to Ryoma's home, then Tabuchi alone should have been enough. Iguchi neither knew where Ryoma lived, nor had any interest. The only reason he was here was because of the boss's order.

Not to mention how Iguchi could be summarized in a single word: a delinquent.

After entering the company through his parents' connections, he was assigned to the rubbish heap that was division three, where he was known for his ill temper and short fuse.

In the documents he submitted for form's sake when entering the company, he had played up his personality as 'dauntless,' but that was just a nice way of putting it. In reality, he simply couldn't read situations, mind his manners, and had no problems vocally expressing his complaints. He had also voiced similar complaints about visiting Ryoma's home this time, grumbling as he demanded early departure as a condition for him to go.

Naturally, the company couldn't send such a person on external projects, so he normally spent his time at the office slacking off on any duties he had. Which was probably why they had chosen him, if it didn't matter whether he was there or not...

Of course they had to pick the one with the worst attitude, and give him approval to leave early... No matter how you look at it, it's an abuse of power.

"...You constipated or something? Don't you look at me, fuck. Your face makes me sick. Turn around."

For the record, Iguchi had been at the company for two years. Tabuchi had been working for longer and was older, but thanks to his connections, Iguchi was higher positioned.

■ ■ ■

"Urgh, what a fuckin' shithole. That old fart lives like this?"

Accompanied by Iguchi, who was uttering insults from the moment they arrived, Tabuchi rang the doorbell of the corner room on the second floor.

But the person they were seeking was no longer in this world.

"...Hey, asshole! Are you deaf?! You can't just skip work unannounced!"

"Please wait, Iguchi. He might not be at home. See, the morning newspaper is still here..."

"Oh? So you're saying he skipped work to go out and fuck around somewhere?"

"He could be hospitalized, or out shopping... Chief lives alone, so he has to look after himself if he gets sick. It looks like we have no choice but to wait..."

"YOU WOT?!"

Iguchi grew even more infuriated.

"Umm… we were ordered to talk to him directly, and the phone wouldn't connect, so we came all the way here…"

"Oh, fuck this… Hey, asshole! I know you're in there! Don't bullshit me!"

"H-Hey, calm down a little…!"

Iguchi raised his voice and banged on the door loudly.

Since he was dressed in a proper suit, it kind of made him look like a loan shark here for collections.

Sensing that something was amiss, an old man's voice traveled up from the bottom of the stairs.

"Excuse me. Do you people have business here?"

"Ah? Just who the hell are you?"

"Sorry for making so much noise! We're coworkers of the person who lives here. We haven't been able to contact him since this morning."

"Takebayashi's coworkers?"

"Yes, do you know him?"

"Let me think… He didn't seem particularly different when I saw him last night."

"Hey. Don't ignore me, you old fuck. I asked, who the hell are you?"

"The landlord."

"Landlord? Perfect. Open this door."

"Don't be ridiculous. I may have a key, but I'm not about to open a tenant's door without prior notice. Are you people really Takebayashi's coworkers?"

"I apologize for the late introduction. My info is all on here."

Tabuchi gave a deep bow as he took his business card out of his pocket and offered it.

"Hmm… Do you like robots?"

"Huh? Y-Yes, I love them."

"He's previously mentioned a subordinate with this family name that liked robots…"

"That's him. We work in the same division as that old man, and this one's a nerd with kiddy hobbies for his age. Now open the door already."

"…Tabuchi aside, this one here doesn't know his manners very well. It's hard to imagine you're a working adult."

"You wanna go, asshole?"

"Iguchi, calm down."

As a hostile mood settled in the air —

"Could you keep it down?!"

The door beside them opened to another person yelling loudly.

"All I've been able to hear for the past few minutes is you people screaming at the top of your lungs! It's a bloody nuisance!"

An unshaved middle-aged man appeared from next door.

He had dark circles under his sleepy eyes as he glared at the three of them.

"I apologize, Urami."

"Oh, *now* you want to apologize after busting in here and making that racket? Tch!"

The man called Urami was still unhappy, but cooled down a little seeing Tabuchi.

"…Just keep it down. And isn't the next door away from home? The walls here are thin so I can hear if someone moves around on the other side."

"I'm so sorry for the trouble. Do you know where…?"

"No clue. Are you sure he's at home at all? The guy who lives there isn't around very often."

"Yes, he should be… He finished work early yesterday and said he was going to read a li— a book."

"Well, dunno then."

"Everything would be hunky-dory if this geezer just opened the door."

With a glance at Iguchi, who was displaying an indignant attitude for the world to see, the man leaned in to whisper to the landlord.

"Landlord, mind if I ask you for a little favor too?"

He had determined that Iguchi wasn't worth talking to.

Thus, to have them return as quickly as possible, the unrelated neighbor also joined in persuading his landlord to open the door.

The four of them argued back and forth over the door for a while.

"Fine…"

Finally, the landlord folded first.

"About time."

"In return, I expect you to leave immediately if Takebayashi is not present."

"Well, no shit."

"I'm sorry, please go ahead."

"Hmph. You must have it tough too."

With a look at Tabuchi, who continually bowed his head, the landlord went to get the key to open the door.

"Takebayashi! Are you here?"

"Yelling here isn't gonna make much difference. Move it."

"?!"

"Whoa! What?"

Iguchi shoved the landlord yelling from the entrance aside, toppling him off balance.

Tabuchi made it in time to support him, but Iguchi paid them no need as he charged inside.

"Hey, old codger!"

As Iguchi jeered from inside the room, the landlord at the entrance similarly raised his voice.

"Just what is with his attitude?!"

"I'm so sorry about him! Are you injured?"

"I'm fine. But really, Tabuchi, what's that kid's problem? You said he was a coworker, but what kind of company would hire a child like him?"

"Umm... I can't say the details, but he had connections into the company..."

"Even with connections, a newbie should mind his manners more, no? There's no part of him that acts like an adult!"

"Stop snoozing and get your ass up!"

Iguchi's voice yelled louder than before.

Tabuchi couldn't help but hear him and reacted in shock, the landlord also forgetting his anger.

"He's sleeping...?"

"So the Chief's here after all."

"Oi! Get up, you piece of shit! Skipping work unannounced, at your age?! You're such a pain in my ass!"

The sound of stomps and jeering could be heard.

"...Let's go inside too, or he might destroy the room."

"Yes..."

When they went inside, they saw...

The man from next door who had gone past them without their notice, standing by the living room wall with a bitter smile on his face.

His gaze was directed at the bedroom, where a large man lay asleep.

And…

"Get up! Are you fucking with me?! I'm gonna have your ass fired!"

Iguchi ripped away the covers and yelled, but when the sleeping man showed no reaction, he lost his temper and kicked him over and over instead.

"H-Hey! You're going too far, Iguchi!"

Tabuchi moved to hold him back in a panic.

"Outta my way, fatass!"

"Guh!"

Unfortunately, he didn't have the strength to stop him by force, and a body blow fueled by irritation was thrust his way.

However…

"Please calm down, there's no need for violence…"

Tabuchi panted harshly, curled up in pain as he slipped into the space between Iguchi and Takebayashi.

"Move it, fatass. I'm waking this asshole up myself."

His face was flushed red with anger as he slowly made a show of raising his fist.

"I'll punch you in your fat mouth this time, you want that?!"

"Be silent, imbecile!"

The one who put a stop to him was — against anyone's expectations — the landlord's fist.

"Oww… What's your problem, you old fuck?!"

"I could ask you the same! Everything that's come out of your mouth is abuse. You've charged right into someone else's home uninvited. You've laid your hands on people as though it's your prerogative. Who in their right mind brought you up like that, anyway?!"

"Y-You wot…?!"

The landlord scolded him like a child, like a stubborn father from a bygone era.

It made even the arrogant Iguchi shrink in on himself, and had enough intimidation to calm the current scene at hand.

"Tabuchi, is Takebayashi okay?"

"Y-Yes! Actually, he's still sleeping...? Chief?"

Tabuchi had been too distracted by Iguchi's fists and the pain lingering in his abdomen to realize something was off until now.

Takebayashi was in a T-shirt and shorts for sleepwear. He was lying face-up in those casual clothes, his left hand placed over his stomach. The way his eyes were closed made him look like he was indeed asleep.

However, could anyone sleep through such noise, on top of being kicked multiple times?

Upon closer inspection, his skin was bruised.

From their long association with each other, Tabuchi knew that Takebayashi's body was much tougher than average.

But he wasn't so thick-headed that he would sleep through bruising kicks.

"Chief? ...Chief?"

With that thought in mind, Tabuchi gradually increased the volume of his voice, but Takebayashi didn't even twitch.

Then, he finally noticed.

As he was watching Takebayashi for a reaction, he saw that his chest wasn't moving up and down.

"...Please wake up!"

At the same time as his pleading shout. He reached a hand out to shake awake the body before him, and —

"It's cold..."

The sensation of a body that had lost its heat and stiffened.

254

Without any room for dispute, it informed Tabuchi that Takebayashi was dead.

■ ■ ■

"Thank you for your assistance."

"Yes…"

After Takebayashi's body was discovered, the landlord immediately called the police and everyone who had been in the room was questioned on the situation.

Although they had been released from the police, the commotion out front had brought out spectators.

To avoid the meddlesome looks from busybodies, Tabuchi dragged his feet heavily to the apartment garden.

"You've worked hard today, Tabuchi."

"Ah, Mr. Landlord."

The landlord stood there, avoiding the crowds like Tabuchi.

"Want a drink?"

"Yes, please."

The landlord suddenly offered a can of tea.

After passing the can over, he looked towards Takebayashi's room that was occupied with busy officers.

"Tabuchi, I'd like to apologize for earlier."

"Huh?"

"Before we entered the room. I vented my complaints about that kid's attitude to you."

"Ah… Don't worry about it. We really were the ones at fault here."

"You must have it rough too. And… I'm sorry about Takebayashi."

"…I expected the Chief to live longer than me."

"As did I. I never imagined he'd be the first to leave…"

A silence fell over the two of them.

"Tabuchi, what will you do now?"

"For now… I have to contact the company. I'm just waiting for Iguchi first."

"That boy still isn't done?"

"Not yet. He said he'd come find me when he was done."

"Let me go, goddammit!"

""?!""

Speak of the devil.

Just as their conversation turned to the topic of Iguchi. Iguchi was brought out of the empty room the landlord had given the police officers to use for questioning, his arms pinned behind his back.

"Iguchi?!"

"Stop right there! Don't come any closer!"

A different officer to the one that had opened the door ran up to Tabuchi to stop him.

"Umm, I'm his coworker. What happened?"

"He flew into a rage in the middle of questioning. Though he's still raging now…"

"Let go of me! I didn't kill him! That codger snuffed it long before I even touched him!"

"All right, all right. We'll listen to the details at the station."

"I said— Hey?! Oi, Tabuchi! Get off your lazy ass and help me!"

"H-Help you how?"

The officer blocking his way shook his head.

"You fucker! Don't forget this! Once I'm out of the can, you're fucking dead!"

"...Take him away."

"Yes, sir!"

After spitting out more self-incriminating remarks, Iguchi was taken to the police car parked out front.

"Umm, what will happen to him?"

"Assault against a police officer. Obstruction of a public servant from their duties. He'll be restrained for a while, but if he calms down then he'll be released in a few days. He did many things to extend his sentence, so unless anything else happens he'll be let off with a fine."

"I see... May I contact my company?"

Thus, Takebayashi's death was reported.

Each relevant place received notice and dealt with it accordingly.

But at the same time...

"Ah, Head Editor. Thanks for picking up, it's Urami. Actually, I found some interesting material just now... Yes, I had my phone hidden while filming. I've sent the clip to you, so if you could have a look at it— Yes. He was just yelling about how he couldn't tell from the socks and muscles... I'll email you the details. I believe there's dirt to be dug up on the man in the clip and his surroundings... Yes, please do. Thank you."

In the commotion leading up to Takebayashi's confirmation of death, there was a reporter who held an interest in Iguchi and his place of employment...

Takebayashi was a man who had been given simple hardships through an act of god.

His workplace and living lifestyle was a cage prepared to keep a beast, so to speak.

However, with no beast to keep, there was no need for the cage, and no need for the environment to be prepared in such a way.

Just like how an enormous dam can collapse from the smallest crack.

With the death of the beast Takebayashi as the catalyst, his company and its employees were unknowingly proceeding down a path of destruction.

～ Afterword ～

First, my gratitude to the readers.

Thank you for purchasing *By the Grace of the Gods 2*.

It is thanks to everyone that the previous volume received a second print right away. And now, following the release of volume 2, volume 3 and the comic version has also been decided.

I've heard that the publishers in charge of me have found my story promising, and I have received many comments and support on the website Shousetsuka ni Narou.

It was a greater reception than I expected up until the release of volume 1, so I was bewildered for about a week.

It truly was a result beyond my expectations. From the bottom of my heart, I am so grateful to the readers.

Now, *By the Grace of the Gods* has already reached the second volume, and I have experienced novelizing twice.

It was a flurry of work during the production period, but looking back on it now... There were many things I didn't know for the first volume, and I had many questions for the editors and publishers as I worked every day. I must have caused much trouble for the editors and proofreaders.

But this time, possibly thanks to my experience last time, it felt like the processes went by more smoothly, and I could feel my own growth.

I won't say I'm used to it, but I'd like to accumulate these small growths and use them in my works in the future. I will work hard to return all the support I have received from everyone.

Dear readers, I hope you continue to enjoy *By the Grace of the Gods*.

Fulfilling a monster subjugation request with top-class adventurers!

Mizelia

Miya

Cilia

Welanna

Date: 10/8/21

GRA ROY V.2
Roy
By the grace of the Gods.

Ryoma
Takebayashi

Jeff

"Earth Fence"

There had been bandits that looked down on me for being a child, but even they hadn't pissed me off as much as the men before me. This may actually be the most irritated I've been since coming to this world.